Caster & Fleet

THE
CASE
OF THE
RUNAWAY
CLIENT

PAULA HARMON
LIZ HEDGECOCK

WHITE
RHINO
BOOKS

ISBN-13: 978-1717792655

For Marie Lloyd

CHAPTER 1
Connie

'You ought to think of my feelings, Constance.'

I paused in the act of reaching for my hat and looked at Mother, who was sitting ramrod-straight in the boudoir armchair. 'I don't understand, Mother. I'm visiting Maria to discuss my dressmaking requirements. I wasn't aware that you had any strong emotions about velvet versus satin, or eau de nil rather than burgundy.'

'That is not what I mean, Constance, and you know it.' I didn't think it was possible for Mother to sit any straighter than she already did, but next to her a poker would have looked as if it were slouching.

'Then what, Mother?' I settled the hat towards the back of my head and tied the ribbons.

'Precisely. What are you going to do about Mr Lamont?'

'I don't think I need to do anything about him.' I inspected myself in the mirror one last time, trying not to look at Mother's reflected frown, and stood up.

'You most certainly do.' Mother stood too. 'Don't

leave, please, I haven't finished.'

I sighed, and submitted, wearing what I hoped was my most patient yet infuriating face.

Mother bristled. It probably didn't help that in my boots I was a good head taller than she was. 'The point is that everyone knows.'

'Knows what?' I said, looking down at her.

'That you and Mr Lamont are —'

'Are what, Mother?'

'*Romantically involved*,' she said, with an expression of utter distaste.

'But I thought that was a good thing,' I said, as innocently as I could. 'Why, Mother, you spent half of last year throwing me in his way. You ought to be pleased.' It was all I could do not to smirk.

'Yes, but it hasn't resulted in anything, has it?' Mother held up her left hand, pointing to her wedding and engagement rings. 'You haven't caught him, have you?'

'Mother, Albert is not a fish. We're still getting to know each other.'

Mother sniffed. 'Given the amount of time you spent whispering together at the D'Arcys', I wouldn't have thought there was much left to learn. People are talking —'

'People are always talking. I don't see why I should manipulate Albert into a proposal — if I could — just because your friends have nothing better to do than gossip. Now if you'll excuse me, Mother, I have an appointment to keep. Otherwise I shall have to become a hermit, as I have simply nothing to wear.' And I left the room without a backward glance.

Maria's workshop was tucked away in the trading area of Pimlico, but close enough to Belgravia for ladies of quality to feel safe when visiting. Even better, Maria had talked the local bobby into a regular patrol outside, aided by a never-ending stream of tea and sandwiches. I made an effort to breathe slowly and deeply as the carriage rattled towards it. I should know better than to let Mother irritate me. At the age of twenty-three I ought to be able to rise above it. But Mother, like an expert fencer, could usually wound me in exactly the right spot.

Until fairly recently her barbs had been loaded with criticism of me as an awkwardly-shaped social embarrassment. Now that I had found a seamstress who could make affordable clothes which suited me — and, more importantly, now that I had a young man interested in me — Mother seemed determined to paint me as a fast young lady who would come to grief. I sighed. Why couldn't she leave me alone and nag one of the others for a change?

'We're here, Miss Connie,' Hodgkins called, and I came to with a jerk. 'Shall I wait?'

'No, thank you,' I said, disembarking. 'I'll get a cab home. Or I might go into town for lunch.'

'Very good, Miss Connie.' He touched his cap.

I climbed the small steps to Maria's workshop and rang the bell. As usual, Maria herself answered the door. 'Miss Swift!' she cried, taking my hand. 'Come in, do.' I heard the carriage wheels creak into life as I stepped over the threshold.

'How is business?' I asked, as we walked down the corridor to Maria's office-cum-workroom.

She looked shy for a moment, then a giggle rose to the surface, like a pan of calm water just beginning to bubble. 'It's wonderful, Miss Swift! Two new clients this week, and three last! I shall need more girls, because mine are working up to the limit — at least, to *my* limit.' Her face darkened for a moment, and she seemed to be looking inside herself, to harder times.

'I'm glad we're keeping you busy,' I said, in an attempt to lighten the mood.

'Oh I'ɪɪɪ not complaining, Miss Swift,' said Maria, ushering me in. 'I wouldn't change it for the world. But I want to make sure I do right by the girls.' Her mouth set in a firm line.

'How are the divided skirts selling?' I asked, as I sat down.

Maria smiled, and I saw a distinct twinkle in her eye. 'They're one of our best lines. The thing is, as soon as one of our customers tries one out, they tell all their cycling friends. Sometimes I've had as many as ten ladies on the doorstep at once, like a group outing, and poor Constable Saunders left in charge of the bikes.'

'I doubt he minds too much.'

'No,' said Maria, thoughtfully. 'The ladies tip rather well, I believe.' Her face brightened. 'Now, what can I do for you, Miss Swift?'

'I would like to order some new gowns, Maria,' I said, pulling a couple of magazines from my bag. 'I need at least three evening dresses, and if you can re-trim them part-way through the season, that would be most helpful.' I sighed. 'It's my sister Veronica's turn to be debutante this year. I did suggest to Mother that she could visit you, but —'

'That's quite all right,' said Maria briskly. 'What style did you have in mind?'

'I thought perhaps something like this?' I opened the first magazine to the fashion plates. 'In cornflower crepe de

Chine?'

'Mm.' Maria drew a notebook towards her and placed her withered hand on the facing page, holding it open. She scribbled busily with the other hand. 'With the same ruching?'

I considered. 'Perhaps a little less. Oh, and the neckline a little higher, please.'

We spent the next twenty minutes or so very happily discussing fabrics and colours and details. 'Would you like us to check your measurements, Miss Swift?' Maria paused, her hand on the book.

I shook my head. 'I'm sure what you have will be accurate.' Indeed, everything I had bought from Maria had fitted perfectly, unlike most of my previous bespoke gowns. They had always been a good inch too narrow, as if no-one could possibly be as large as I.

'Wonderful.' Maria closed her order book with her good hand. 'Would you care to see the workroom before you go?'

'I'd love to,' I said. 'So long as I don't disturb anyone. I'd hate to cause a crooked frill.'

Maria laughed. 'I doubt it.'

She led the way to a door with a glass panel, from behind which came a buzzing like the sound of a thousand industrious bees. She opened it to reveal a large, light room with rows of work-tables. There must have been twenty women in there, sewing with machines, cutting out fabric at the large back table, fitting garments onto tailor's dummies, or hand-finishing clothes. 'They're doing so well,' she said, quietly.

I surveyed the scene. 'I don't remember this room being so big,' I said.

Maria shook her head, grinning. 'We expanded into the storeroom when the new girls came. Miss Gregory's delighted.' She put her hand on my arm. 'You must tell Miss Demeray to come and see it, Miss Swift.'

'I certainly shall. Don't forget to send your bill in, Maria.'

I took my leave and walked to the cab rank two streets away. I had planned to have lunch with Katherine Demeray in town, but a note had arrived from her in the first post. *Sorry but can't come to lunch. I have something which I need to do today. K.*

So here I was, my business complete, and no-one to lunch with. A little imp sitting on my shoulder whispered that if I wired Albert, he would almost certainly come into town and take me somewhere nice —

But no. After this morning's conversation with Mother, the last thing I wanted to do was give her ammunition for further lectures. I knew better than to think she wouldn't find out. I occasionally wondered, in fact, whether Mother had somehow convinced her friends to spy on me; the number of times I ran into one of them on Oxford Street, or in the park, or at a gallery or concert, was astonishing. Then again, we all moved in the same small sphere, and it was only since meeting Katherine that I had learnt there was a life outside those encircling walls. Mother thought it was beyond the pale; but often I thought the same about Mother.

I reached the cab rank, and minutes later I was heading into the city.

You could still wire him, said the imp.

I'll probably see someone I know in town, I fought back. *If I run across him in town, that's different.*

'Where to in town, ma'am?' called the cabman.

'Simpson's in the Strand, please.'

That's his favourite restaurant, the imp remarked.

I like it too, I replied.

Of course. The imp bowed, and disappeared in a puff of smoke.

The maitre d' hurried forward. 'Miss Swift! How lovely to see you. I'll take you to your table. Mr Lamont hasn't been waiting long.'

I restricted myself to 'Thank you,' although my brain was whirring as fast as one of Maria's sewing machines. The maitre d' escorted me towards a corner table, and there was Albert, looking entirely at home, toying with a small glass of sherry. He stood when he saw me, and bowed over my hand. I tried not to think of the imp.

'This isn't a coincidence, is it?' I asked, under cover of the menu.

'Well,' he said, stretching his long legs, 'not really. I called at yours to see if you'd like a drive out, as it's such a nice day, and your mother said you weren't at home. She looked quite huffy about it, too.' He winced into his sherry. 'So as she didn't say you were with anyone, I thought you'd probably be heading into town, and you might want lunch. And here we are.' He looked very pleased with himself, and drained the remainder of his sherry.

'Yes,' I said. 'Here we are.'

CHAPTER 2
Katherine

I sat in Father's chair with the tattered letter I'd received in November. Was it trying to tell me something beyond the obvious? All these months of working out the worries of Dr Farquhar's clients, and I had never looked very hard at my own father's letter with its incomplete news and vague sense of foreboding. Connie had asked me to join her for lunch but I felt jumpy today, and my discomfort would express itself as temper which was unfair on my best friend. It would be better to go into work on my day off and take my mood out on a typewriter. I was holding the letter up to the window when the doorbell rang.

Moments later Aunt Alice, dressed to go out, entered the study.

'You have a visitor, dear,' she said, 'and I do wish he made a little more sense.'

Ah. James. His constant teasing of me baffled Aunt Alice and she was never sure if she needed to stay for propriety or not.

I followed her into the hall.

'Will you, will it…' she started.

'Madam means,' said Ada, walking past with a duster, 'if she goes out can she trust you not to get up to shenanigans?'

I stifled the urge to ask if we could trust Aunt Alice. I knew perfectly well from her pink cheeks and lowered glance that she was meeting a gentleman for morning coffee. Which particular gentleman from the cycling club was anyone's guess. She was divulging nothing at present.

'I promise,' I said, ushering her out of the door, 'if you promise too.'

Aunt Alice gave me a bashful frown and scuttled down the steps.

'Could you bring us tea and biscuits, Ada,' I said and entered the drawing room.

James rose from the chair by the cold fireplace. His kiss was brief and he stepped back to contemplate me. I reached up to my hair. It was in a long, loose untidy plait.

'You look like a painting. Ophelia perhaps,' he said. Then he seemed to shake himself. 'But more alive.'

I opened my mouth to retort but saw he was making a statement rather than a joke. I sat on the sofa. He sat back in the chair. What was wrong? It was unlike him. Even with the threat of invasion by the rest of the household, he generally sat next to me and held my hand under the edge of my skirts.

It was not only Aunt Alice he baffled. While Connie and my cousin Albert were so besotted I wanted to bang their heads together, James just teased me. Yet his kisses were warm and ardent. Or at least they had been until today.

'Any absorbing puzzles to untangle recently?' he said.

9

I shrugged. 'A few. Any interesting injustices to investigate?'

'A lot.' He looked into the fire, then back at me. 'What's that in your hand?'

'It's the letter Father sent three years ago; the one which arrived last November. I wondered if there might be a hidden message, although it's just his usual rambling.'

'You must miss him,' said James. I thought he would put his arm around me, but he stayed distant. 'It must be very hard not knowing what has happened to them.'

'Yes. It is,' I closed my eyes. If Father never returned, I would never stop wondering. It was exhausting. 'I keep hoping another letter will arrive, or a report, or something. But it's more than four years since they left, and still nothing.'

'Was it just your father who wrote?'

I looked up, startled. Henry's note releasing me from any vague 'understanding' was long consigned to the fire.

'His secretary Henry wrote too.'

'You'll be glad when they come back.'

'Of course I shall.' I frowned. What an odd thing to say.

'Henry too.'

'Well, of course.'

'And when Henry does return…'

'James, what is all this about?'

'I hadn't realised you were engaged to him, Katherine.'

I blinked. I was about to go to him when Ada walked in with the tea. She looked with approval at the distance between us and put the tray down on the low table. I waited till she'd gone. 'James, who said that?'

'It doesn't matter. You should have told me yourself.'

'But it's not true.'

He looked at me properly.

'We were never engaged,' I said, 'never. Henry and I . . . I can't explain it. He worked for Father. He and I discussed things. He expressed a fondness for me. He kissed me on the cheek before he went away. I can't even remember how I felt about him. I was young and no man had ever shown any interest in me.'

James snorted.

'It's true.'

'They must have been blind.'

'Who?'

'You're very pretty.'

'You're the one who must be blind. I'm scrawny and carroty and have freckles.'

He was silent again, neither agreeing nor contradicting. A cold feeling went through me. Had he kissed me because I was there, unchaperoned, easy prey? Perhaps he had never intended anything by them, any more than Henry had. I felt my face grow warm.

'James, if —'

The doorbell rang and Ada clattered up the hall.

'If you think I'm the sort of woman who —'

'Telegram, Miss Kitty,' said Ada, shoving it into my hand. 'Answer?'

I scanned its contents.

New client STOP Fancy your name in lights QUERY Farquhar STOP.

I looked at the clock and turned to Ada. 'Tell the boy the reply is "arriving noon",' I said, and handed her some coins.

James stood up. 'If you need to be there at twelve, I won't detain you.' He looked at my hair, and a flicker of

11

his usual manner twinkled in his eyes. 'It will take you an hour to tame that mop for a start.'

'Wait!' I said, rising. 'James, please wait. Drink some tea, eat a biscuit. I shall be twenty minutes at most. Besides, you haven't seen my new hat.'

'I hope it's not the new fashionable type with a bird's posterior stuck on top.'

'Wait and see.'

He hesitated. Something in his face looked lost.

'You're a good journalist,' I said, stepping closer. 'You'd never write a story without listening to both sides. You'd always give weight to the person you trusted best.'

'True,' he said, after another pause. He checked his pocket watch. 'I'll time you. In ten minutes I'll hail a cab. If you're ready when it arrives, we'll go together and talk.'

***

I was back downstairs by the time James was standing on the threshold. I might yearn for the frills and flounces that Connie could carry off, but even if they had suited me, that sort of dress would have taken a lot longer to put on than my simple green outfit with black ribbon in a Grecian trim and a double row of buttons. The sleeves were puffed just enough to be in proportion to my height, and the bodice shaped and boned to make me look as if I had a bust. James followed me down the steps and handed me to the cab, where I sat jamming the last pins through the hat and my coiled-up plait with the same force a farrier would use to shoe a horse.

'Harley Street, please,' James told the driver. It was a relief to be going by cab. I usually had to travel by omnibus.

'See, no feathers,' I said, pointing at my hat, which

billowed with ribbons.

'Mmm,' said James. 'I'd love to see you with your hair down.'

'I'm not fifteen.'

James sat opposite me and looked out of the window.

'Are you really not engaged?'

'No. When I was younger than Connie is now, Henry was quite attentive. There was nothing more than that. Perhaps I assumed something more. But as I say, no-one else had ever shown any sort of interest. Father's letter included a note from Henry telling me I was nothing more to him than his employer's daughter.'

James coughed. 'How did you feel?'

'Honestly? By then, I felt relieved. Humiliated. In equal measures.'

'Fool.'

'You asked.'

'I mean Henry.'

James got up and sat next to me. His arm came round my shoulders.

'Besides,' I put my chin up and pretended he wasn't stroking my cheek. 'I never knew you cared.'

'It seems I do,' he said, and turned my face to his. I was glad I had used so many hat pins.

In no time, the cab lurched to a halt.

'Damn,' said James. 'The good doctor lives too close. Do you want me to come in with you and find out what anxieties your client faces today? A poodle with the vapours? A handkerchief returned from the laundry with someone else's monogram? Mysterious chalk marks on the front wall?'

I detached myself from him and opened the door.

13

'Don't be facetious. When is the deadline for your article?'

James sighed, leaned out of the cab and gave the driver the *Chronicle*'s address.

'I hate it when you're right,' he said. 'Will you dine with me tomorrow?'

'Maybe,' I said. 'It depends on the severity of the poodle's vapours.'

I smoothed my dress, straightened my hat and rang Dr Farquhar's bell. As the cab rattled away, I realised that James had not said who told him I was engaged to Henry.

***

I waited in the vestibule, watching the to and fro of patients and trying to guess their ailments. From outside came the rumble of traffic, bird-song, children. A hurdy-gurdy man started playing nearby. I was trying to work out the tune he was playing when the doctor's manservant Mallory came to collect me.

'Ah, Miss Demeray,' said Dr Farquhar as if surprised to see me. 'You don't normally work today. Oh, of course, you're here about Mr Templeton. Now let me find…'

He rummaged in the papers on his desk. Part of me itched to reorganise them, but it was bad enough typing up his memoirs. I had my own room on an upper floor, marginally bigger than a broom cupboard, where I transcribed Dr Farquhar's notes or interviewed those of his clients whose complaints were related to anxiety. I mostly provided reassurance, a little investigation and a listening ear. It wasn't terribly exciting, but it was better than six days in a government office.

'Is he not here?' I asked.

'Mm? Oh no. He couldn't persuade his protégée to

14

attend. I took some notes and thought you could go to speak with them at his . . . ha ha . . . place of work. I expect you'll like that.' He continued rummaging.

I wondered what on earth he meant. 'Dr...'

'Ah, here they are.' Dr Farquhar readjusted his pince-nez. 'Mr Templeton is acutely anxious about *goings on* with his protégée...'

'I'm not sure I...'

'He is concerned for the reputation . . . ha ha . . . of his business. Nothing is quite as it seems.' He took off his pince-nez. 'Smoke and mirrors, my dear girl, smoke and mirrors.' He laughed uproariously and then seemed to register my bafflement. 'I forget that you have slipped back into a sheltered life, my dear. Maiden aunts and afternoon tea, I imagine. But a change is as good as a rest and I am sure you are old enough to go to the music hall without having to ask permission, provided you have a suitable escort.'

'The music hall?' In my head I saw bare legs and red velvet. I heard the bounce and clash of loud irreverent tunes and scandalous songs. I had only once been to anything more lively than a church concert.

'Yes,' the doctor continued. 'Mr Templeton manages the Merrymakers Music Hall.' He paused. 'Perhaps you could take Miss Swift. She was looking a bit dreamy last time I saw her. A visit to the music hall would be better than a tonic. Her mother won't approve, of course. However, I have great hope of you, Miss Demeray. If anyone can find a way to sneak her out, it is you.'

He handed me his notes and smiled. 'I look forward to your report.'

15

CHAPTER 3
Connie

I had no idea that Wednesday was *the* day to lunch at Simpson's. By the time Albert and I finished our main courses, we had already been accosted by several of our acquaintance. Albert seemed perfectly at ease; but I could feel myself fidgeting more and more as first Maisie Frobisher and her mother, then Harold D'Arcy, then Delia Carroll, came up to our table to exchange pleasantries. After upsetting my water-glass, I put my hands in my lap and kept them there.

'I thought I'd find you here!' The words made me groan; but the voice did not. I turned in my seat and found my eyes almost on a level with Katherine Demeray's.

'Another puzzle solved,' I said, as lightly as I could.

'Well,' Katherine replied as the waiter hurried to place a chair for her, 'it was hardly difficult. I'd cancelled our lunch today, and knowing you, I thought you'd still want a treat.' She raised her eyebrows at Albert, who, while apparently engrossed in the menu, raised a languid hand.

'I thought you were working,' I said, in an attempt to

divert her.

'I am,' said Katherine. 'And so are you.' She had a gleam in her eye which I recognised, though I hadn't seen it for months: the gleam of a woman on the trail of a mystery.

'Tell me.'

'I w —' The waiter bustled over to hand Katherine a menu. 'I've already dined,' she said. 'Maybe coffee.'

'Of course, madam.' The waiter looked inquiringly at me and Albert.

'Just coffee for me too, thank you,' I said, hastily.

Albert considered. 'Plum pudding and custard, please,' he said, eventually.

'Very good sir, madam.'

'Where does it all go?' said Katherine, eyeing Albert's slender frame.

He grinned. 'Hollow legs, K.'

'It isn't fair,' I said. 'I'll probably gain weight just by watching you eat it.'

'Share it with me, then,' he said. 'You might as well get some benefit from it. And the portions are generous.'

'That's why I ordered coffee,' said Katherine. 'I wouldn't want to investigate on a full stomach.'

'Come on then,' I said. 'What are *we* investigating?'

Katherine scanned the vicinity to make sure no-one was within earshot. 'The mysterious ailment of a music-hall star.'

'*What?*'

'Your coffee, ladies,' said the waiter, setting it down before Katherine and me. 'I will return with your pudding, sir.'

'Jolly good,' said Albert, and the waiter glided off.

'Since when have you two qualified as doctors?' he said, under his breath.

'Very funny, Albert.' Katherine stirred sugar into her coffee. 'Dr Farquhar asked me — us — to investigate because he feels this case requires a woman's touch. She wouldn't even come to his rooms.' She broke off as returning footsteps indicated the arrival of Albert's pudding, which was lowered onto the table.

'Good heavens,' I said, as Behemoth descended.

'Don't worry,' said Albert, picking up his spoon. 'I intend to take it slowly.'

'Carry on,' I said to Katherine, turning my chair away from the pudding. 'I need something to distract me.'

'All right.' Katherine opened her bag and took out a sheet of paper, folded twice. She opened it and smoothed it out on the table, between us. 'This is what Dr Farquhar gave me.'

I peered at the writing, but Dr Farquhar's writing exhibited the key medical characteristic of illegibility. 'You'll have to translate it for me. I can't make head or tail of it.'

'I'll give you the gist.' Katherine leaned forward. 'Our actual client is a Mr Templeton, who manages the Merrymakers Music Hall in Lambeth. But the person we're interested in is his' — she scrutinised the paper — '*main attraction*.' Her finger underlined the words. 'He wouldn't give the doctor her stage name, but her real name's Ellen Howe.'

'He wouldn't give her stage name?' I mused as I sipped my coffee. 'Isn't that the wrong way round?'

Katherine considered while trying her coffee. 'One would have thought so,' she said. 'But I suppose he wants to keep her stage name quiet. That's who the public know her as.'

'So what's wrong?' I asked. 'If it is a proper illness, there isn't much we can do except try to persuade her to visit Dr Farquhar.'

Katherine's eyes scanned the scrawled lines. 'It's…' She glanced round again. 'Like most of the cases Dr Farquhar asks me to help with, there's clear evidence of anxiety and nerves. Here we are.' She found her place, and read. 'Client says she has died on stage twice.' She looked up. 'I think that means she "froze". Miss Howe ran off the second time, and refused to go on at all the following night. She did not give an explanation, saying that she forgot her lines. Miss Howe was persuaded back on stage the night afterwards, and her performance, while nervous at first, was normal. This continued until the matinée on Saturday afternoon, when she ran offstage again.'

'How strange,' I said.

'If you're going to have any of this,' said Albert, rather thickly, 'you'd better hurry up.'

I swivelled round and gasped at the near-empty bowl. Albert wiped his mouth with the napkin, and scraped the last of the plum pudding onto his spoon. 'It was lovely, but I'm full. Come on, help me out, Connie. I can't insult the chef.'

The spoon advanced towards me, and I sighed. 'Oh, all right. If I must.' Albert held his napkin under the spoon, and steered it carefully into my mouth.

A shocked '*Well!*' almost made me spit the pudding out. The dowager Lady Bartington was glaring at me. As soon as my eyes met hers, she huffed and made a show of turning away.

'Oh no,' I muttered. 'She's bound to call on Mother.'

'I'll go and explain,' said Albert, unfolding himself from his chair. Even with a three-course lunch inside him, he still managed to move gracefully.

Katherine nudged me. 'Stop gawping at him,' she whispered.

'I wasn't,' I protested.

'Oh yes you were.'

'Fine.' I turned my chair round.

She sighed. 'I do wish you two would just get married and have done with it.'

'Don't you start.' I frowned into the dregs of my coffee. 'Mother's already reprimanded me today for failure in my duty.'

'I'm sorry.' She laid her hand on mine. 'It isn't any of my business…' She looked down. 'But we would be related.'

'He's got to ask me first,' I snapped. Just then a high, wheezing laugh rang out behind me. 'At the moment, he's busy charming Lady Bartington.'

'Getting you out of trouble, you mean,' Katherine replied. 'Anyway, I'm pulling you lovebirds apart for a few hours. We have work to do.'

'Excellent,' I said, resolutely not looking round. 'Couldn't be happier.'

***

The exterior of the Merrymakers Music Hall did not live up to its name. It was a plain, square, down-at-heel building, standing a little apart from its neighbours as though they had offended it — or it had offended them. The only clue to its purpose was the two large playbills posted on either side of the double doors.

'*EXCLUSIVE TO THE MERRYMAKERS!*' the playbill screamed, '*LITTLE DOTTIE JONES! VOICE OF AN ANGEL!*' The other acts crouched beneath, in type of descending size.

'Are you going in, or what?' asked the cabman. 'I'm not hanging round waiting. And neither should you,' he added.

'We're going in,' said Katherine, and pulled me after her.

The foyer was dark and cheerless, and the ticket booth was empty. Presently we heard whistling, and a young lad with a broom came through the door marked *Auditorium*. He stopped dead at sight of us. 'We ain't open,' he said, leaning on the broom.

'I know,' said Katherine, drawing herself up. 'We've come to see Mr Templeton. Dr Farquhar sent us.'

'Doctor Farkar, eh?' he sing-songed, smirking. 'Well, if Doctor Far-kar sent yer, I'll make sure 'e knows.' He leaned his broom against the wall and strolled off, resuming the whistle.

He was back in less than a minute, the smirk gone. 'This way, ladies.'

Mr Templeton's office was tucked behind the ticket booth. The lad knocked, and vanished. 'Come in!' resounded from within.

On the other side of a large desk was a man in a check suit, smoking a cigar. A newspaper lay before him. 'Afternoon,' he said, removing his cigar. He stood up to shake hands, and did not gain much in height by doing it. 'I'm Dick Templeton, manager, proprietor and master of ceremonies at the Merrymakers. I take it you're here about my top of the bill?'

21

'We are, yes,' said Katherine, shaking his hand.

'And do you have names?'

I glanced at Katherine. 'Yes,' she said, smiling. 'I am Miss Caster, and this is Miss Fleet.'

'Caster an' Fleet, eh?' His eyes shone like jet beads. 'Big an' Small, more like. You'd make an excellent comic turn.' The room was stiflingly hot, and I hoped my face wasn't as red and shiny as it felt.

'Thank you,' said Katherine. 'I think we'll leave the entertainment to you.'

'Only a bit of fun,' he said, winking. 'Now, you've managed to turn up at a good time. Usually Ellen wouldn't come in till gone five o'clock. Theatrical folk sleep late, you see, due to being up till all hours, and she ain't no exception. But Wednesdays, we re'earse. *Ron!*' The last word was delivered at such volume that I winced.

The young lad appeared. 'Yes, Mr T?' he said, mildly.

'Watch out for Ellen, and when she shows up, tell her to get in 'ere.'

'Sir.'

The door closed, and Mr Templeton winked again. 'I do a bit of ventriloquiz too,' he said, opening his desk drawer. '*Like this*,' came from the interior, and I giggled. 'Sometimes I tease young Ron by talking from behind him. Drives him nuts, it does.'

'Mr Templeton,' said Katherine, laying her notes on the desk. 'Before Miss Howe arrives, is there anything else we should know? Anything you haven't already said to Dr Farquhar?'

Mr Templeton pondered, chewing on his cigar. 'I don't think so,' he said. 'Ellen's not the confiding type. Close as an oyster, she is. I doubt any of the girls know what she's thinking. But on stage, she's worth her weight in gold.' He grinned. 'Given the size of 'er, that ain't so much. Ha!' He smacked the desk in self-appreciation. 'Might use that, it's a good 'un.'

Suddenly he stiffened, his eyes fixed on a point somewhere outside the room. I could hear the faint, regular tap of heels on a hard floor. 'And if I ain't mistaken, that's Ellen coming now.'

Chapter 4
Katherine

Mr Templeton leaned back in his chair and smirked. His face went still, but I was conscious of a low vibration, and his stiff collar moved. From somewhere outside the room a voice called 'Wotcher Ellen, tell Ron to hurry up with the rosie and come in 'ere.'

The footsteps slowed, stopped, then came closer. The door opened and a small figure in cerise entered.

I am often taken for a child because of my size and lack of curves, but it was not just that Ellen was short; it was her demeanour. She hovered on the threshold like a timid little girl, twisting her right foot. Her hair was loose and her dress would have been appropriate for a child of twelve. Its skirt stopped half way down her calves, revealing thin ankles and buttoned boots.

When she stepped into the room, however, it was clear she was old enough to be putting her hair up and kicking out her hems.

'I wish you wouldn't do that, Mr T,' she said. Her voice was West Country, soft and leisurely, as if she had all the time in the world to speak.

'You love it really,' said Mr Templeton. 'Nah then, I want you to meet these ladies. Miss Caster and Miss Fleet.'

'Are you a new act?' Ellen ran her eyes over us, gauging our height difference which wasn't as marked while we sat, taking in our clothes and frowning.

'See,' said Mr Templeton, 'Ellen knows a good stage name when she hears it. What could you two do? Miss Fleet, I'm sure you have hidden talents.'

A set of confused reactions ran across Connie's face before she managed to force it into neutrality. He must have hit a nerve.

'As for you, Miss Caster,' Mr Templeton leant forward and exhaled cigar smoke without removing the cigar, 'don't suppose you'd do me a favour. Stand up and shake hands.'

There was something mesmerising about him, and I found myself standing eye to eye with Ellen Howe, her hand in mine.

'You could be sisters!'

Ellen and I looked at each other and then round at Mr Templeton. My hair was red and curly, Ellen's was black and smooth as a raven's wing. Judging by the roots showing at her hairline, I suspected her hair was naturally mousy brown. My eyes were green, hers a startling blue. Our faces were different shapes, hers round as a child's, mine high-cheeked. But we were both small and slender.

'Maybe not close up, but on stage anything can be true! Fancy your name in lights, Miss Caster?'

I felt a frisson which made me understand Connie's earlier expression. Did I? I shook my head and smiled at Ellen. She narrowed her eyes.

25

'Miss Caster's here to see if she can help you get your nerve back.'

'My nerve is fine, Mr T,' said Ellen, dropping my hand, 'I've come to rehearse, ent I?' She stepped out of the room as Ron came in with the tea.

'Give her a bit of time,' said Mr Templeton. He puffed out another lungful of cigar smoke and I wondered how I would explain the odour on my clothes to Aunt Alice. Perhaps it would blow away before I got home.

'When was the last time you two saw something on the stage, then?'

'Father took me to see Mr Irving play Mephistopheles in *Faust* when I was just a girl,' said Connie, as if she was fifty. 'It was so thrilling. Lightning and everything. And two years ago, I saw Miss Terry as Lady Macbe —'

'I'm sure that was wonderful,' interrupted Mr Templeton, 'and you, Miss Caster?'

I squirmed. The theatre hadn't appealed to Father, who preferred classical concerts, and what I'd thought of as Henry's restrained courtship had consisted of his requesting I accompany both of them to scientific lectures.

'I very much enjoyed listening to talks by F... Roderick Demeray.'

'Froderick?'

'I . . . nearly said Frederick.'

'I remember. Well, he sailed into the unknown a good while ago,' said Mr Templeton, 'but I'll own he was a good performer. I wonder if the whole disappearance thing was a set-up to cause a sensation when he does come back. Although he's leaving it a bit late, now...'

He appraised me through the smoke and I pretended I was Connie to keep my face neutral.

26

'Come on then, ladies,' he said, rising, 'come and have a butchers at Ellen's act.'

The music hall wasn't quite what I had expected. The upper levels were much the same as in a theatre, including private boxes and curved rows of seats. The auditorium, however, was like a restaurant, with evenly spaced tables, a bar, and chairs facing the stage.

We sat with Mr Templeton at the table nearest the orchestra pit, as Ellen sang song after song, skipping across the stage. The songs ranged from light, silly stuff about toys, pets and childish worries, to melancholy as her voice trembled in recollection of a dead mother, then to saucy as she pretended to be a little sister spying on her elder sister's trysts. There was a great deal of light innuendo in the 'child's' misunderstanding of what she saw but it was so cleverly done as to be funny rather than sordid.

Her voice, a light soprano, was utterly beautiful. Every word was clear, whispers audible, grief pulling at your heart one moment, tears of laughter coming to your eyes the next. And she could act. Looking at her on the stage you would think she was barely twelve, whereas in real life, I was fairly sure she was at least my age. Maybe nearer thirty.

As she made her exit, Mr Templeton muttered 'Wait 'ere a minute,' and left us surrounded by empty, smoky plush seats and gilt caryatids. A few moments later, he appeared on stage carrying a life-sized dummy, and sat on a chair with it on his lap. The dummy was of a boy, with bare feet, ragged breeches, a loose shirt and an oversized man's cap. Articulated arms and legs jerked and whirled at Mr Templeton's behest, and its jaw moved as if it spoke while Mr Templeton's ventriloquism kept up a steady flow of risqué jokes and observations. I wondered whether Ellen would join us, so that I could talk to her.

'What do you reckon then?' said a voice behind me. We turned but no-one was there. Looking back at the stage, we saw Mr Templeton laugh and stand up, letting the dummy slide from his lap. But instead of clattering to the boards, the dummy landed neatly on its feet and made a bow, sweeping off the cap to allow long black hair to fall. Ellen straightened at our applause, lifted her nose and marched off. Mr Templeton ran down the steps at the side of the stage and came up to us.

'Dunno what to say, ladies,' he said, 'but I got my doubts she's as tops as she says she is. Tell yer what. I'll get you tickets to come tonight and see the show for real. The whole shebang. I'll get you four tickets cos I daresay you're not allowed out without an escort and to be honest girls, I don't think you'd be wise to come without. There'll be plenty of gents in my audience but they'll be gents full of drink. And a gent full of drink is just a man. So four tickets it is. We'll see 'ow it goes later, shall we?'

***

At home, I hung my green outfit in front of the open window to try and get the smoke out of it, and opened my trunk. Wrapped in tissue and lavender was my one and only evening dress. Shaking it out, I smoothed the rosy silk and remembered. Six years ago, when I was twenty years old, the Lamonts had invited us to a ball. Aunt Alice had demurred on the grounds that she must stay at home with my ten year old sister Margaret. I had been so excited to order a dress which had no function but to be beautiful. Aunt Alice had tutted over the lack of sleeves, the modestly low neckline, and the frivolous swags and loops of material in the skirt, but Father, seeing my delight, had approved it. And Aunt Alice, doubtless thinking of the eligible young men who would be dancing with me, finally withdrew her objections. Now I hung it on the wardrobe door and compared it with the fashion plate in today's ladies' magazine. My sewing skills were reasonable, but without Aunt Alice's help I couldn't remove all the excess frills and furbelows from the skirt and bring it up to date. Even Aunt Alice might not be able to do it in two hours.

Margaret walked in.

'You're not going out in that, are you?' she said. 'It's so out of style.'

'I'll have a long cloak over it, no-one will notice.'

Margaret snorted.

'Do your teachers let you make that noise?'

'They're not here.' Her eyes narrowed. 'Where *are* you going, anyway?'

'I'm going . . . out with Connie.'

'Ooh fancy,' said Margaret. 'Well, you'll look ridiculous next to her. All her dresses are right up to the minute.'

I ignored her and peered at the superfluous trimmings. At least there weren't as many frills as I'd have liked originally, so it wasn't as fussy as it might have been, but it was still a long way from the sleek modern lines. The frills were firmly sewn in. If I cut them off, would that work? No, it would look worse. And it would drag on the floor without a bustle. Perhaps I should just let Connie go without me and ask her to report back tomorrow. I could deal with whatever she discovered when I had something fashionable to wear.

'You'd have to be stupid to go out in that,' repeated

Margaret.

'Or brave.' I put my head up and gritted my teeth. I would be brave.

'I'm glad I won't be seen with you.'

I ignored her and turned attention to my hair. Pinning my plait up in a hurry in the morning meant that what James had called a mop then was a rat's nest now. There was no time to do anything with the dress when I only had two hours to deal with my hair. I hoped James knew so little about fashion that he didn't realise how out of date I was.

But I had to go, whether I looked ridiculous or not. Mr Templeton was right, I knew it. Underneath the defiance, Ellen Howe, stage name Little Dottie Jones, was a very frightened woman, and it was up to us to find out why.

Chapter 5
Connie

'We're early, aren't we?' asked Albert, sticking his head out of the carriage window. 'I thought the show started at half past seven.'

'It does,' said Katherine. 'Connie and I need time to talk to our client beforehand, though.' Her voice was clipped and precise, and she kept her cloak bundled round her. I had taken care to change into one of last season's dresses; partly because I did not want to risk a new one in what might be a crowded and spill-ridden environment, and partly because I'd never heard Katherine mention an evening dress, and I didn't want to show off. I saw her looking sidelong at my outfit more than once, and hoped it passed muster.

'The doors are open,' said James, opening the carriage doors and handing us out. 'Let's go and get ourselves settled.'

The Merrymakers Music Hall had come alive. The lamps in the foyer blazed, and Ron, now resplendent in a dress-shirt and bow tie, stood in the ticket booth, barking his wares. 'Come and see the show! No fewer than eight — *eight* — acts on tonight's bill, INCLUDING the famous Little Dottie Jones! Jerry Jerrold the fantastical juggler! The wit and wisdom of Dan Datchett! And Betty Tanner and her Wonder Dog!'

'I can hardly wait,' said James, advancing with the tickets.

''Ello ladies,' said Ron, leering at us. 'My, we are fine tonight, aren't we?'

Perhaps I was imagining it, but I had the distinct impression of a scowl crossing Katherine's face. However, it was gone as quickly as it came, and she said 'Good evening, Ron' most civilly.

'A private box!' Ron exclaimed. 'Oh, aren't we in the money! Now, if you noble folk would like a drink, you can place your order at the bar and the waitress will be round with them later. When you're ready, you're in number six: through that door and up the stairs.' He grinned, and transferred his attention to the next customer.

'You two go and do — whatever you want to do,' Katherine instructed. 'We're heading backstage.'

James clicked his heels, saluted, and grinned.

'Are you all right?' I asked Katherine, as we headed down the corridor marked with a pointing finger and the word *Artistes*.

'Yes, I'm fine,' she said, tossing her head. 'Why wouldn't I be?'

It would have been easy to find the performers even without a sign. As we progressed, the smell of sweat, resin, and cheap perfume grew stronger and stronger, the threadbare carpet petered out, and the walls grew stained and marked.

32

Katherine knocked on the door marked *Ladies*, and it was wrenched open by a woman in her stockings and corset, but fully made up in a style which would be visible from the highest box; black-rimmed eyes and scarlet lips. 'Whaddayer want? It ain't curtain up for another forty minutes.'

'Doesn't the show start at half past seven?' I asked.

She grinned. 'You're green, aintcher? The later we get going, the more drink the bar can shift.' I shuddered, and more than ever felt glad that Albert and James had accompanied us.

'Anyway, what *do* yer want? Cos fans go to the stage door, see.'

'They're here to check up on me,' said a voice behind the door. 'Ent that so?' Ellen wore the same girlish dress as earlier; but now her hair was tied in two bunches with matching cerise bows. Her eyelids were blue and bright pink circles had appeared on her cheeks.

'How are you feeling, Miss Howe?' asked Katherine.

'Miss Howe!' shrieked the first woman. 'We '*ave* gone up in the world! Ellen 'Owe, wiv a title!' She ran the name together: Ell'nOw.

'I'm all right,' said Ellen. 'Bit nervous, bit excited, just like usual. Get yourselves in, you're making a draught.' The door opened wider to admit us.

The large room seemed small, crammed as it was with women in all stages of dress, rails of costumes, and an assortment of shabby tables littered with sticks of paint, powder puffs, brushes and hairpins. It was a huge, busy dressing-up box.

Ellen led us to the quietest corner, and indicated a group of rickety chairs. 'There ent nothing wrong with me,' she said, in an undertone. 'Mister Pernickety expects perfection, and if he don't get it, he cuts up rough. I only forgot a line or two.'

Katherine opened her bag and consulted Dr Farquhar's notes. 'But this says you've run off stage twice.'

'I ent seeing no doctor.' Ellen's little hands clenched into fists, and under the paint she looked like a defiant child. 'He can't make me. I'm the draw here, and if I go —'

'He'll find someone else,' said another woman, loudly, as she skewered pins into her hair. 'You're only as good as yer last performance. One day you'll be too old to play the child, EllenOw, an' then you'll be out on yer ear like the last one. Oo bothers about Daisy Chalmers now, eh?'

'Shut yer trap, Betty,' said Ellen, in a matter-of-fact way that suggested it wasn't the first time the remark had been made. 'I ain't going nowhere. And I ain't seeing no doc. There.' She stared at us with round china-blue eyes. 'You'd better get out. Some of us have work to do.'

'I hope the show goes well,' I said, as we stood up.

'Would yer look at that frock!' Betty shouted, pointing at Katherine. 'Did yer buy it off Mrs Noah? Cos it's out of the ark!'

Raucous laughter enveloped us. I took Katherine's arm and steered her out of the room before she could say anything.

'Don't mind them,' I whispered in the corridor. 'There's nothing wrong with your dress, and it's a lovely colour.'

Katherine stared at me, then stamped her foot and walked off, pulling her cloak round her. I hurried after her, but her raised shoulders and brisk gait showed me more clearly than words that speaking to her just now would be unwise. She tended to cry when angry, and that always made her even more furious.

We climbed the stairs in silence, listening to the growing noise beneath. A long corridor opened in front of us, with doors on the right hand side. Box six was the last.

Albert and James were already seated, and looked remarkably cheerful. On the table were four pints of beer, two half-drunk, and two small glasses of red wine. 'Hope that's all right,' said Albert, looking anxious.

'Have you had your chat?' James asked Katherine.

She nodded, and sat next to him.

'Aren't you staying?' He touched her cloak, but she smacked his hand away.

'Yes. I'm cold.' Katherine stared over the edge of the box to the stage.

Albert raised his eyebrows at me, and I shook my head. 'You've missed half the fun,' he said, gesturing at the crowds in the stalls. 'They've already broken up two fights.'

It seemed as if the show would never begin, and that we would be doomed to stay in that box forever, sipping sour wine and listening to the singing, shouting and catcalls below. But at last the small orchestra struck up a reedy tune, and Mr Templeton stepped out from behind the curtain. He had acquired red cheeks, black eyebrows, and a top hat since our last meeting.

'Ladies and gentlemen!' he roared. 'Have we got a show for you tonight! All yer old favourites, and of course, Little Dottie Jones!'

The audience cheered, stamped, and whistled its approval till Mr Templeton held up a hand for silence.

''Old yer 'orses! Save it for the acts!' He laughed loud and long, and the audience joined in. 'And wivout more ado . . . it's Jerry Jerrold and his amazin' balls!' Ribald laughter followed him offstage, and the curtain rose to reveal a tall, thin man juggling.

Act followed act, greeted with shouts, cheers, and occasional boos. Some of the performers had difficulty in making themselves heard over the conversation of the audience, and the clink of glasses. But a great cheer arose when Ellen popped her head round the curtain. ''Ello!' she said, grinning. 'Did you miss me?'

The audience welcomed her with aahs and exclamations.

'Ain't she lovely?'

'Marry me, Dottie!'

'You can sit on *my* knee any time you like!'

She took their comments with good humour, and gave them a couple of songs. 'I'll see you later, everyone!' she cried, blowing kisses to the audience.

'Is that your one?' asked Albert. 'She seemed perfectly all right to me.'

'Yes,' I said absently. 'She did, didn't she?' I had watched her closely throughout, and beyond a sharp glance towards the boxes, she had been completely focused on pleasing the audience. Perhaps she was right, and it was excessive zeal on the part of exacting Mr Templeton.

The next few acts came and went, including a lewd comedian who I supposed must be Dan Datchett, and a luckless operatic tenor who was booed soundly the moment he opened his mouth. 'Not you again! Get Dottie back on!' yelled a heckler. The singer looked embarrassed, but persisted despite being almost completely inaudible over the din. When he was followed by a troupe of female acrobats in very skimpy costumes, several men stood up for a better view.

The acrobats left the stage to groans and whistles, and there was a slight delay before Mr Templeton appeared. He was slightly out of breath, but grinning. 'You caught me unawares, ladies, I barely 'ad time to put me telescope away!' He let the audience laugh. 'An' now we have Betty Tanner and Buster, the Wonder Doooooooooog!'

There was muttering from the audience, but they subsided as the curtain rose and Betty stepped forward with a tan and white fox terrier. 'Say hello, Buster!' she cried, and he barked, twice.

Two minutes into their act I heard a soft tap at the door, and Mr Templeton poked his head round it. 'Miss Caster,' he said, his eyes focusing on Katherine, 'could I trouble you for a word? I would welcome your assistance.'

'Of course,' said Katherine quietly, and got up. If anything, she seemed pleased to leave. She had barely looked at James since we had entered the box, which in itself was unusual.

'Should I come too?' I asked.

Mr Templeton looked at me as if he had never seen me before. 'Er, no, no thank you. Miss Caster's all I need. Come along, dear.' The door closed behind them.

I sipped my wine carefully as Betty put Buster through his paces. He walked on his hind legs, performed somersaults, and even spelt out his own name with the aid of some large cardboard letters laid on the stage. Then he danced to music from the orchestra. The audience were growing restive, and Betty kept glancing into the wings. *Ellen must have had another wobble*, I thought.

37

Katherine's talking her round in the dressing room. I hoped she would manage to solve whatever the problem was, as the discontented buzz below was growing louder and louder.

Suddenly Betty gestured to the band and shouted 'Thank you, everyone!', her face a concentrated beam of relief. Polite applause broke out, and everyone cheered as Mr Templeton came back on.

'I've only come to say a quick 'ello,' he confided to the audience. 'I'm 'avin a terrible time with me dummy today. You won't believe what he's gone and done this time!'

'Wot's he done?' shouted the delighted audience.

'Wait till you see 'im!' bellowed Mr Templeton, walking to the wings, where scuffling could be held distinctly. ''E's dressed up as a girl!' He vanished, and reappeared a moment later carrying his life-sized dummy, its limbs dangling — only this time, instead of ragged breeches and a dirty shirt, the dummy wore a frilly pink evening dress, teamed with the usual oversized cap. The dummy also wore a mutinous expression underneath its mask of pink cheeks, blue eyelids, and bright red mouth. I blinked, and stared harder.

The audience roared with laughter.

'Don't he look pretty?' The dummy's mouth stayed resolutely down. 'Come on, give the audience a wave.'

The dummy didn't move, so Mr Templeton lifted its hand and did the job himself. 'See 'ow grumpy he is?'

'Hello, everyone!' piped the dummy's still mouth.

'Hello!' the audience shouted back.

'That's better!' shouted Mr Templeton, and waved the dummy's hand more extravagantly. It caught the brim of the cap, which flew off, revealing a head of auburn hair.

The audience went wild. 'Look! Carrots!'

James's mouth fell open. 'What the —' He stood up, and hurried from the box, his face black as thunder. His footsteps thudded down the corridor.

Albert turned to me. 'Did you know K was going to do this?' he asked, frowning.

'Of course not!' I cried. 'She's been forced into it! She must have!'

I made myself look at the stage. The audience were singing a sentimental song along with the dummy, whose eyes were fixed on our box. 'Oo, he's upset!' somebody shouted, in mock concern. And even from this far away, I could see the utter mortification on the dummy's painted face.

CHAPTER 6
Katherine

Outside the box Mr Templeton had dropped his posh accent and a little of his bluster.

'Ellen's done a runner again,' he said, running his hand over his face. 'She's due on in ten minutes and when the punters find aht there's gonna be trouble.'

I reached for the door-handle. I needed Connie to help talk to the performers, and maybe the men could start a search.

'Nah,' said Mr Templeton putting his hand on my arm. 'One o' you's enough for the mo. Those girls're twitchy as a bunch of cats on a bed o' nails. I dunno if they'll talk to you. But maybe one of 'em can tell you where she is . . . maybe she's 'iding out back. I just gotta do the ventriloquiz act. That's all. Come on.' He took my elbow and led me down the stairs.

'Of course I'll talk to them.' I wished Connie was with me. The women in the changing room might take better to her. 'I'm sure the act will be perfectly good with Ellen's understudy.'

'Yeah, if she didn't 'ave the quinsy.' Mr Templeton ushered me through the building to the backstage area. Someone was singing on stage. It sounded so different; muffled, other-worldly. 'Or more likely she's got man trouble. Oo knows. Women. Always let yer dahn.' I waited for him to apologise but he didn't. 'Do yer worst,' he said, knocking at the ladies' dressing room door and opening it for me.

'You after Ellen?' snapped Betty. 'Long gorn. Whatever it is to you.'

The others paused in various poses, changing outfits, doing their hair, painting their faces. They gave me the cold stare of an opposing team or perhaps army, then turned away. But one, a slip of a thing aged about twenty, came close as she went to pass through the door and whispered. 'She saw something out in the audience. It spooked 'er good and proper.' She was gone before I could ask any more.

'Huh,' said Mr Templeton. 'I thought you was gonna solve my problems and I ain't sure you ain't made 'em worse. Although…' He looked me up and down. 'You look game. Are you game? I need a dummy. Not the full act. I can pretend you've got the lurgy and ain't yerself. Are you up for it? Wot you reckon?'

I swallowed. Going on stage? Me? I hadn't done anything like that since school. Yet I felt I was letting him down, as well as Dr Farquhar. All I had to do was sit there and let him do the talking. That wouldn't be hard. And no-one would know it was me. I gave a tiny nod.

'Stout fellah!' said Mr Templeton, pushing me back through the door. ''Ere girls, as none o' you's prepared to do it, Miss C's offered to be the dummy. Get 'er ready.

You got two minutes.'

But there wasn't time to get me changed into the boy's outfit. The women laughed and twisted me about, pulling at my dress and saying the hooks were stuck, smearing paint on my face, giggling.

'These furbelows won't budge, she's too proper!' yelled Betty.

And Mr Templeton shouted back: 'She'll be orl right. Just stick the cap on and send her aht.'

I was stiff and awkward in his arms through sheer panic. And then we were on stage, the lights glaring in my face and jeer after jeer after jeer and the rest became a blur.

***

There was a serious flaw in my upbringing. I had been loved, nurtured, fed, educated and knew right from wrong, but no-one had ever thought to teach me how to swear.

It hadn't mattered until the moment I got off that stage, when I could have done with every single curse available to express my feelings.

I stumbled through the wings, past the smirking dancing painted girls in their short skirts and feathers, who were lined up to twirl onto the stage. The principal dancer, grinning, pulled out some of my hairpins before I could stop her. Half my hair fell down in a mess of curls, and blinded by hair, pain and humiliation, I stumbled into James's arms.

At least he was able to express himself in a steady flow of obscenity. His warm hands were on my bare arms but I didn't care. I felt as rigid as the dummy I was supposed to be.

Mr Templeton ambled up behind me as a rhythmic heavy clop on the boards drowned the music from the orchestra pit.

'Who's this then? Your knight in shining armour? Still,' he went on, lighting a cigar, 'you did the trick Miss Caster, gotta hand it to yer. Thanking you kindly. You kept the show on the road, so to speak.'

'How could you make her do it?' James had found his voice. His fingers gripped my arms more tightly than I suspect he intended and I wriggled my way out of his embrace. I couldn't see my cloak anywhere. I wiped my eyes on my glove, looked in revulsion at the paint and took a deep breath.

'Whoa there, Sir Galahad,' said Mr Templeton, 'I didn't make her do nothing. I told her the trouble and asked her nicely to help. She coulda said no, but she said yes. You're game ain't ya, Miss Caster? I can see it don't come natural, but I reckon you've got it in you. If you ever change your mind, I could train you up for the stage.'

'I never knew it would be like that!' I cried, and despite Mr Templeton's nonchalance, he took half a step back when I glared at him.

'What trouble requires you to make a mockery of a lady?' snapped James.

'Ellen's gone and 'opped it.'

'What's that to my . . . my young lady?'

'Your financy, or whatever she is, offered to sort out Ellen's nerves. Only it don't seem to have worked yet.'

'Maybe —' My voice squeaked, and I paused to compose myself. 'Maybe she doesn't like pretending to be a child. Maybe she doesn't like pretending to be a boy. Maybe she doesn't like pretending to be a puppet controlled by someone else.'

Mr Templeton inhaled his cigar deeply. On stage, the

43

clomping of the dancers stopped and they ran past me. One pulled out more of my hairpins. A rattling overhead and a series of thuds indicated the curtain must have come down. Yells of 'Encore! Encore!' could be heard, and performers straightened coats and dresses ready to go on stage. Another rattle, and the curtain presumably rose. The tenor started a rousing number and the volume of the audience joining in drowned out any calls for Dottie until it seemed as if the whole world was singing along.

'You've got an 'andful 'ere Sir Galahad, and no mistake,' Mr Templeton said to James. 'You take her on proper, you'll need all the armour you can get.' He turned to me. 'Now see here, Miss Caster, no-one's made Ellen do nothing she don't want to. She's got the voice of an angel. She coulda come to me in any guise she wanted and I'd 'ave taken her on. She was the one what chose to perform as a child. Not me.'

He leaned closer, as if to confide a secret. 'See, I've got my eye on the long game. I'm worried her voice will outlast her face if you take my meaning. But then, the stage is sorta magic. You do it right, the audience'll believe anything. Now the ventriloquiz act, that's something else. Wanna know the truth? Used to be Ron what played the dummy. Before him, I had a real dummy, but it got burnt in a fire and I had to improv and it was a bit of a laugh to use Ron. Then Ron got a bit big to sit on my knee and Ellen turned up, and she offered to take it on.'

Mr Templeton stabbed his cigar at me. 'You seem to think it's all my idea, but it weren't. It was 'ers. Suits me, cos it makes money. Minute it don't make money, she'll have to change 'er act. Dr Farkar reckoned maybe you could find out what was bothering her but so far you ain't.

Now she's done a runner and I don't know whether to expect her back tomorrer or not. Her understudy's off sick. And on topper that, one of my stagehands dropped a block on 'is foot this evening and got laid up, so what with one thing and another, I'm pretty cheesed off.'

'Well —'

'And it's no good drawing yourself up to look tall when you're knee 'igh to a grasshopper. I'm used to dealing with women who knew more about the world at five years old than you'll know at fifty.'

'Nevertheless,' I persisted, 'I am very sorry I was unable to help Miss Howe. She was adamant all was well. Perhaps, if you think there is someone who will understand her better, you should ask them to help. In the meanwhile, I'd like to take my cloak and go home. Thank you for a *delightful* evening.'

I swept round with as much dignity as I could and marched towards the dressing room. My cloak was gone.

I slammed the door behind me. 'The thieving . . . thieving…'

'Bastards,' said James, taking my arm.

I shook him off. 'Thank you, I'll find my own bad words.'

I slipped back into the dressing room and grabbed a pot of cold cream while the women clustered round each other, removing their costumes and chatting. James and I came out into the alleyway behind the stage door. It was dark. Men were hanging about, stepping forward as I appeared. James grabbed my arm again and drew me into the shadows. 'Keep your head down,' he whispered. 'You don't want anyone to recognise you.'

We found Connie and Albert on the pavement outside.

Connie was wringing her hands. I'd often imagined the four of us going out for the evening. It would involve culture, good food, sparkling wine, fashionable dresses, laughter, maybe words of love in candlelight. I knew, deep down, that in a week or two my face would no longer burn, but right now I hated all of them. Connie in last year's dress, pitying me, James with his pointless chivalry, Albert with his vague bafflement.

I hunched in a corner of the cab, wiping off the paint with the cold cream and Connie's handkerchief while I stared out at the night. It was high summer, the sky was a warm darkness, stars almost visible. I picked at my lovely, lovely dress. It was beautiful. It was just old fashioned. One day, perhaps, someone would look at a dress like this and gasp at the prettiness, the work that had gone into it, the elegance. They'd dream of a young woman spinning in a ballroom, gazing into the eyes of a young man who was about to propose. They wouldn't ever imagine a woman sitting on a stranger's knee pretending to be a ventriloquist's dummy.

'Have my jacket,' said James.

I ignored him. His arm tried to reach round my shoulders but I squashed them into the corner of the coach.

'All this bare flesh and you're even harder to get hold of than usual,' he whispered, 'but at least your hair's down.'

'Do you have to make a joke of everything?' I snapped back.

'Have my cloak,' said Connie. 'It's a woman's one, it won't be so obvious when you go home. I'll hopefully manage to get in without seeing Mother and if I do, I'll tell her I left it at the restaurant I told her we went to.'

I groaned.

James reached for my hand. It's hard to not let someone hold your hand but I did my best.

He used his other hand to move my hair and whispered into my ear. 'You look beautiful. Even angry. You look beautiful.'

I wondered how much beer he'd drunk. All I could hear was him saying 'what's that to my . . . my...' His what? What was I to him? He'd never said. Perhaps I was just a woman to kiss in a cab.

'Can I borrow some hairpins?' I asked Connie.

She rummaged under her hat and handed over enough pins for both of us to have something approaching a respectable hairstyle.

They dropped me off first. I made them. I managed to get to my room without anyone seeing me and at least when Margaret came in to ask how the evening had gone, it seemed reasonable that I should be brushing my hair with the correct one hundred strokes.

To my surprise, she came to give me a hug.

'I'm glad you went out,' she whispered, 'I'm sorry for what I said. I could see you were upset about the dress and I was so horrid. I'd forgotten what it was like not to have a choice of what to wear. Next time, tell them to give you time to get a new dress first.'

I hugged her back. My little sister was growing up. I could feel the tears returning, and let them flow in silence.

She took the hairbrush from me and carried on brushing my hair.

'I'm sure James didn't notice what you were wearing,' she whispered. 'He only ever looks at you. Connie wouldn't ever care, she's so lovely. And you could wear a bathing suit as far as Albert's concerned; he would be too busy gawping at Connie to realise. Please don't cry.'

'I had a job and I couldn't do it,' I whispered.

'Never mind,' she said. 'It doesn't matter.'

I kissed her and sent her back to bed before Aunt Alice came to tell us both off. It did matter. I was a failure.

The following morning I woke feeling achy and miserable. I remembered how rude I'd been to my best friends and wished I could run away and never come back. I didn't want to face them ever again. While we were at breakfast, the postman delivered a letter from James.

…I'd like to visit you but I have to go out this evening. I have an obligation to meet someone at Paddington which may have a bearing on your investigation. If it does, I'll let you know.

I have a feeling that something I said last night made everything worse but I'm not sure what. Contrary to what people say about redheads, the rose-pink suited you. If anyone tries to make a fool of you again I shall deal with them myself. Although given the expression on your face last night, it might be worse for them if I left you to it. Chin up.

'Well I never,' said Aunt Alice, showing me the newspaper. 'It looks as if a lady must have fallen in the Thames at Lambeth.'

'What?' I said.

'Look, it says they've not found a body but a lady's cloak's been washed up. Not any old thing, very smart. The mark says it was made by Maria's workshop.'

'Really?' I grabbed the newspaper. It was impossible to be sure, but…

'It looks so much like yours,' said Aunt Alice. 'How very curious.'

I had a job and I couldn't do it. And it did matter. I had to pick up the pieces of myself and start again.

CHAPTER 7
Connie

Ada stood on the doorstep and glared at me. 'Yes, Miss Kitty is in, but she said she wanted a quiet morning. I'm not surprised, after last night's shenanigans. She was like a bear with a sore head at breakfast.'

'Please, Ada,' I wheedled.

'Who is it, Ada?' Katherine's voice, but lower and tired-sounding.

'It's Miss Swift,' Ada called back.

'Come in, Connie,' said Katherine.

Ada swung the door open with an air that no good would come of it. 'Don't overtax her,' she warned, and stomped off. 'I suppose you want tea,' she flung over her shoulder.

Katherine took me up to her bedroom and we sat, me in the little armchair, her on the bed. 'Are you all right?' I ventured.

She shrugged.

'Albert's very worried about you, you know. He even sent a note this morning, asking me to call and see how you were. I mean, I was going to call, anyway.'

Katherine rolled her eyes. 'If he's so concerned, he could have sent me a note. I'm not contagious.'

'No, of course not,' I began, and then couldn't think of anything else to say. I couldn't tell her how twitchy James had been on the journey to my house, or how quiet Albert was. Or how he had kissed me before opening the carriage door. Definitely not that…

'Have you seen the newspaper?' asked Katherine, and I shook my head.

'What's happened?' I asked, but she had already gone to find it.

I looked around the little, quaint room, with its flower-sprigged wallpaper and white painted furniture. In the corner was a trunk, and flung across it, as if asleep, was the rose-pink dress.

I jumped at the click of the door. 'I never want to wear that again.' Katherine dropped the paper in my lap. 'Page four.'

I turned to the page, and read:

SUSPECTED DROWNING AT LAMBETH

A lady's cloak has been found washed up by Lambeth Bridge. It was spotted late last night by a man walking his dog, who alerted police.

As yet no body has been found, but we have been informed that a search will be conducted later today.

The cloak has been removed to Lambeth police station. Members of the public are encouraged to come forward if they saw anything last night which might have a bearing on the case.

The item in the sketch below looked very familiar. I looked up at her. 'Will you go and get it?'

Katherine bit her lip. 'I can't afford to lose a perfectly good cloak because of some idiot's practical joke. Ellen didn't take it — it disappeared while I was on stage.' She looked up at me. 'But I don't particularly want to advertise where I was last night.' She blinked, and her eyes were wet.

I moved to sit beside her. 'We can go together.'

'Would you — would you go with me?'

I put an arm round her. 'Of course. We won't go anywhere near the music hall.'

'It was horrible,' she whispered.

'Try not to think about it,' I soothed.

'You don't understand,' she said, twisting her hands in her lap. 'It was too late to back out. Or perhaps it wasn't, but I didn't want to let him down. He told me I was made for the stage and it would be fine. But all those people staring and jeering. I felt such a fool. It was a nightmare.' She shivered. 'If I wasn't proud . . . if I'd had time to prepare . . . if I could have worn the boy's outfit, maybe… oh I don't know. It's all a blur. And James *saw* me like that.' She put her head in her hands.

'Yes, but . . . he still loves you,' I said, to the top of her head.

'Does he?' was the muffled reply.

'He came to rescue you, didn't he? And he tried to make you feel better, all the way home.'

'I suppose.' She looked up with a watery smile. 'But couldn't he just tell me?'

My gaze followed hers to the crumpled dress in the corner. 'We'll take it to Maria,' I said. 'She'll be able to alter it for you, and bring it up to date, and then you can wear it again without thinking about —'

She shuddered. 'Perhaps.'

***

After a restorative cup of tea, we bundled the dress up and hailed a cab. Maria stroked the rose-pink silk like a favourite cat, and Katherine's face brightened a little. 'Can you do anything with it?' she asked.

'I certainly can,' said Maria. 'There's so much material. I can remove most of the frills, take the fullness out of the skirt, and maybe add some contrasting trim —'

'It'll look like a different dress,' said Katherine. 'Good. That's what I want.' Then her face clouded. 'How much would you —'

'My treat,' I said hastily. 'Call it a late extra birthday present.' I would have paid twice whatever Maria's price was to put a smile back on Katherine's face, after what she had endured the night before.

***

'And you say someone took it?' The police officer looked at us suspiciously. Katherine's cloak lay on the desk like a dead body, emitting a musty dampness in the warm room. 'Did they steal it?'

'I think they took it from a cloakroom by mistake,' said Katherine.

'And threw it in the river,' he finished off.

'Maybe they were drunk,' I added.

He glared at me, then drew a line in his notebook. 'No body's been found, and the cloak's been claimed, so it's a happy ending.'

'Yes, indeed,' I said. 'We won't take up any more of your time, officer.'

53

His eyes were level with mine. 'No, madam, you won't.'

***

There were no cabs to be had from the police station. 'Let's walk to the main road,' I said, 'we can probably catch a cab there.'

Katherine nodded, but as we walked a familiar, square building came into view, and she clutched my arm. 'Let's find another way,' she said.

We changed direction and cut down a side street, but it led to a maze of smaller roads. 'Katherine,' I said gently. 'I think we have to go that way.'

Her grip tightened. 'I'm not crossing the road. I'd rather walk all the way home.'

Her pace slowed as we approached the building. 'There's a cab coming now,' I said. I stuck out my free arm to hail it, and tried to step forward, but Katherine held me back.

'*Look*. Come on, I've changed my mind.'

Across the road, Ron was ripping down the playbills.

'Well look 'oo it is,' he said, as we approached him. 'If it ain't Lady Muck an' the dummy!' Katherine's fingers dug so sharply into my arm that I felt as if it might come off.

'What happened?' I asked.

'Our leading lady's 'ooked it,' he said, laconically.

'I knew that last night,' Katherine retorted.

'No, I mean she's *really* 'ooked it,' said Ron, peeling a long strip of paper away. 'A note came for Mr T this mornin' and she ain't comin' back. You shoulda heard him swear when he read it! I learnt a few new ones, I can tell you.'

'She's not coming back?' asked Katherine.

'Naow.' Ron looked her up and down. 'So if you did fancy reprisin' your act, you've turned up at the right time.'

'Shut up, Ron,' said Katherine, dragging me through the doors. 'Just shut up.'

***

'Didn't think I'd be seeing you again,' said Mr Templeton. 'Decided you like it after all, eh?'

'No,' said Katherine, firmly. 'I happened to be passing, and Ron told me the news.'

''Appened to be passing,' he chuckled. 'Pull the other one, it's got bells on.'

Katherine put her hands on the desk. 'What did the note say?'

'You can read it if you like.' He opened the drawer and threw a small pink envelope on the desk. *For the attenshun of Mr Templeton*, in a neat round hand. 'Didn't even know she could write,' he observed. 'G'wan, open it.'

Dear Mr Templeton,

I am writing to let you know that I am retiring from the stage. I will not be coming back, and you can't perswade me. Thank you for giving me the chance, and I will miss you all.

Yours sinserly,
Ellen Howe
(Dottie Jones)

'That's it,' he said, taking the letter back. 'Three years, and she ups and goes just like that.'

'You don't seem too upset, Mr Templeton,' said

Katherine.

'I ain't.' He grinned. 'Now if she'd gone off to one of me rivals, I'd be steaming. Or if she'd broken her leg or somefink, that would have been vurry in-con-venient. But as you ladies well know, she'd got unreliable. Fine one minute, running out on me the next. An' when acts is unreliable, that's the worst. Now Raimundo, that tenor of mine, he's mediocre. I could probably go outside and chuck a stone, and 'it a better singer. But he comes in on time, every time, fills his spot on the bill, and 'e sticks it out. Not like Miss Fly-By-Night. An' even *you* —' he pointed at Katherine. 'You did yer time on my knee, though I could tell you hated it. So I'll put Betty top of the bill for now, and see if I can poach a new act from somewhere.'

'There wasn't an address on the letter,' said Katherine. 'Do you know where Ellen lives, Mr Templeton?'

His eyes narrowed. 'What yer saying? I've got a wife and kiddies, yer know.'

'She didn't mean it like that,' I said hastily. 'Would the other — ladies know?'

'They might, I s'pose,' said Mr Templeton, opening his cigar box. 'If you want, you can ask 'em when they get in. Won't be till six at the earliest, though. Now if you don't mind, I've got a leading lady to find and a dummy to replace. *Ron!* Fetch me a copy of *The Stage*, we've got work to do.'

'What do you think?' I asked Katherine, as we emerged blinking into the sunshine.

'Honestly?' She shook her head. 'I don't know. I'd like to talk to James about it, but he's on a mission tonight. I'm not sure he has much time to talk. Perhaps I could go with him.'

'I don't suppose it matters now.' I shielded my eyes and peered into the distance. 'If Ellen isn't working there any more then she isn't Dr Farquhar's case, or ours.' I spied a cab and waved frantically.

Katherine muttered something I didn't quite catch. 'Excuse me?' I asked, leaning down.

She looked up at me, and her face was full of doubt. 'I'm not so sure.'

Chapter 8
Katherine

'You're not coming tonight, Katherine,' James repeated. 'It's a job for the *Chronicle* and I can't take you with me.'

'You can't hint that it concerns Ellen and then expect me not to come,' I argued.

'Concentrate on finding out what you can from the music hall,' he retorted. 'They're women. You're women. Talk. It's what you're all best at.'

'They won't speak to us,' I said as calmly as I could. 'Whatever it is they know, they're not telling it to two, er "hoity-toity misses who think they can take our jobs".'

'Hoity-toity misses' hadn't been the words they'd used, but the principle was the same. I could feel myself reddening under James's grin. I wasn't sure which aspect of their description amused him most, or which he'd like to put right. He sobered. 'It's dangerous, Katherine. Seriously. It's no place for a lady.'

'Neither is Mr Templeton's knee, but I survived. If you don't take us, we'll follow.'

'I give up. You can come, but only you, and only if you

dress the part. We'll get you something in Petticoat Lane. But before you go there, you'd best put on the shabbiest clothes you've got.'

Ada stood sentinel at the front door. 'You are *not* going out like that, Miss Kitty,' she said, eyeing my worn dress. 'People will think we've fallen on hard times.'

I raised an eyebrow.

'At least put a coat on,' she said. 'Your father's coat would hide it.'

'But it's such a warm evening,' I said. 'And even if it wasn't I'd look ridiculous.'

'Better ridiculous than impoverished.' She pursed her lips as I fought my way into Father's enormous coat. 'I'm not going to ask why you're dressed like that. I'd rather not know. Just don't let next door's Elsie see you. I've had enough of her little jibes about your gallivanting.' She opened the door, where a cab stood waiting. 'But stay safe, Miss Kitty,' she added in a whisper.

I shed the coat in the cab and sat opposite James.

'Can't I wear this?' I said.

James looked me up and down.

'You still look like a lady,' he said. 'It's too fancy. Trust me. Although, I prefer it to what you generally wear. It looks more comfortable, less starchy and a lot more approachable.'

He got up to sit down next to me. I rose and crossed to the other side.

'I wish you'd tell me what I've done,' he said.

I shrugged. Now was not the time for the discussion. 'It's too hot,' I said. 'Why won't you bring Connie to Petticoat Lane?'

'I didn't want to take *you* but you made me. At least

59

you know what housework is and have the clothes for it, so, you'll just about fit in. I'm not taking someone who thinks last season's clothes are old. Do you know why they call it Petticoat Lane?'

'Huguenot refugees like my ancestors sold lace for petticoats there.'

'That's one theory. The other is that they can steal your petticoat at one end and sell it to you at the other.'

'How could they do that without you noticing?'

'Don't stand still for too long, in case you find out.'

***

I had never been anywhere like it. It was a sea of dusty people from the stalls on one side of the street to the stalls on the other. I clasped Father's coat like a shield and James anchored my arm firmly in the crook of his elbow. Within seconds I could see nothing. People, their odour: a mixture of perspiration, bergamot, tobacco and cabbage ebbed and flowed as my face pressed against coat after jacket after dress. I stumbled and a woman caught my hand. Hers was rough, rougher than Ada's. I couldn't tell if she'd been trying to help or trying to pick my pocket. Then she was gone. James and I disentangled ourselves from the flow half-way along the lane. I felt as if I had been through a mangle.

'All underwear present and correct?' whispered James. 'I can check if you like.'

We stood at a busy stall. Clothes hung from rails and poles. They were mostly respectably black, worn, and desperately out of date. By comparison, my rose evening dress was positively fresh from the fashion plate.

'Take your pick,' said James. I pointed at a dress which looked approximately my size and hoped no-one had died

60

in it.

'It's just as well Connie can't come, there's nothing for her.'

''Ere,' said the stall holder to me, 'you selling that coat? We could come to a bargain.'

I held Father's ridiculous old-fashioned coat away from myself and looked at it.

I shook my head. Not yet. Besides, if I came home without it, Ada would disown me.

***

A few hours later, at Paddington, we waited in the dusk for the last trains to come up from the West Country and Wales.

'I don't understand why we're here,' I said.

'You didn't have to come,' said James.

'I'm not the delicate little flower you think I am.'

'I don't. You're not Connie.'

No-one ever thought I was a delicate flower. It was a little depressing. But there was no point pouting in the dark when he couldn't see, even if he'd have paid attention. I felt bedraggled in a thirty-year-old dress and a patched paisley shawl as I stood beside James.

'Since you are here,' he said, 'I can show you where Ellen probably started from. It might give you an idea what the trouble is.

He paused. The look in his face was the one I'd seen when he was trying to protect Maria. 'If I can help anyone, I do,' he said. ' It breaks your heart.'

'What does?' I said. 'It's a railway station, people come up to the city for work rather than starve in the countryside. That's quite sensible, isn't it? I'm sure Ada did something like that. She makes a lot more money with us than she

61

could have in the country. That seems wise, not heartbreaking.'

'Watch,' said James.

Night was falling more rapidly now. Out of the shadowy alleyways round the station, small groups emerged. Young women strolled, men lolled, older women with cheery faces stepped into the streetlight and paused.

From the station, the last passengers appeared: sooty, weary, overwhelmed by the city before them.

Among them, a lad with a knapsack darted into the shadows and a shadow followed. Then a girl with a small reticule peered out and hesitated at the entrance. She was perhaps fourteen, tearful.

'I suspect Ellen was like that once,' whispered James. 'And then there was what you said at the music hall.'

'When?' I cast my mind back to the awful evening I'd been trying to obliterate.

'During Ellen's act, near the end.'

James's voice was low, barely audible. I followed his gaze. Three separate people, two women and a man were heading, apparently by accident, towards the girl.

'What —'

'Shh. We might have to help.'

'Who?'

'Shh.'

The younger woman increased her pace and addressed the girl. We were too distant to hear what she said, but she seemed to be imploring her. The girl was hesitating. The other two figures closed in. The older woman appeared to wheedle. The young man, spinning something that glinted, moved in from the other side. The girl started to cry; then she turned to the younger woman and allowed herself to be led off. The old woman and young man, while still appearing to be strangers, exchanged glances and dissolved into the shadows.

'Well done, Angela,' James murmured. 'She'll be safe now.'

'Who —'

'She works for a charity that helps lost girls. It's dangerous work. The girls run away from home thinking it'll solve all their problems and they find themselves in even worse trouble. The people who want, shall we say, to offer them employment don't always take too kindly to losing potential income. You see, there's more than one kind of welcome waiting in London. I write about it in *The Chronicle,* but no one wants to hear it. No one wants to waste money on people they see as wastrels. But I'll keep trying. Anyway, chances are Ellen Howe turned up in London like this. Looking for a better life? Running away? Who knows.'

'Couldn't you have just told us all this?' I asked.

'I was coming here anyway. I'm waiting for someone. You're the one who insisted on coming, and before you ask, it would have been no good dressed as Miss Tea-Party, like you usually are.'

'I beg your —'

'You'd stand out like a sore thumb and bring a completely different set of trouble. '

'Forget all that,' I interrupted. 'What did I say at the music hall? I don't recall saying anything.'

'You remarked on how lovely Ellen's voice was. Then you asked what the audience were laughing at when she made an innuendo, then went as pink as the tiny amount of your dress that you let me see, and then you leant forward

63

and frowned harder. I mean, you were frowning anyway and I still don't know why.'

'Never mind, go on.'

'Then you said "Her voice has changed". I thought you meant she was getting tired, but you didn't, did you?'

I'd forgotten but he was right. I closed my eyes and forced myself back to that evening. We were sitting so close, the four of us, and I was hot. I wanted to remove my cloak, but was too embarrassed. 'Little Dottie' was in full flood and then . . . then her voice did change. There was a tremble in it. She missed a beat in her dancing. Then she recovered herself and became, if anything, more childish. A caricature. Then she skipped offstage.

'She was looking into the audience.'

'Isn't that what you're supposed to do?' said James.

'No, but she was looking for someone. And when she found them, that's when the change happened.'

'If we knew where they were sitting, maybe we could establish who it was.'

'You can only work that out from the stage,' said James. 'You have to go back, whether you like it or not. Now hush a minute and I don't mean to be rude, but can you stand out of the light. I must speak to these people.'

A middle-aged couple and a small boy were leaving the station. They seemed worn out from travelling. The woman looked close to tears and the little boy was actively crying, rubbing smuts deeper into his exhausted eyes. James went up to them and held out his hand.

'I'm Mr King,' he said, 'and you must be Mr and Mrs Johns. Don't despair. We've found your daughter and she's safe.'

'Is she…' Mr Johns swallowed, 'is she in the family

way, like we suspected?'

'Yes.'

'I wish she'd told us,' wailed Mrs Johns. 'She didn't need to run away.'

'She's safe,' repeated James, 'I'll take you to her. We've found you somewhere to stay for the night, and tomorrow morning we'll help you all to go home. Now, young man,' he knelt down by the little boy and touched the side of his head. 'What's this? How long have you been keeping money in your ears?' He opened his palm and displayed a sixpence. The little boy stopped crying and gawked.

***

The following morning, I met Connie for tea and told her what I'd learnt.

'I hope I didn't miss any excitement,' she said.

'It wasn't like that.' I closed my eyes and saw a James I hadn't appreciated, trying to change lives. No wonder he made jokes all the time. He'd seen me into a cab and shot off into the night, without a kiss, without saying when I'd see him again. But he'd given me an idea.

'What are you plotting?' said Connie.

'We need an act,' I said.

'An act?'

'Yes.'

'We?'

'Yes, you and me. I don't see why I should have all the fun.'

'Will it involve — clothes like the ones Ellen wears on stage?' Connie wrinkled her nose.

'Who knows. It could be worse.'

'How could it be worse?'

'I'll explain when I've worked it out. But first we're going to get Reg a job at the music hall. It's not just women who talk.'

CHAPTER 9
Connie

'The music hall?' said Reg, his eyes wide as saucers. 'You're taking me to the music hall?'

'That's right,' said Katherine, with a grin. 'Where better to go for an afternoon's entertainment than a matinee at the music hall?'

'I ain't complaining,' said Reg, quickly. 'Which one?'

'The Merrymakers, at Lambeth.'

Reg whistled. 'That's a fair step. Why not Drury Lane?'

Katherine and I exchanged glances. 'It's, um, complicated.'

A slow smile dawned on Reg's face. 'It's a case, ain't it? We're on another case, ain't we?'

I waved a cab down and we piled in. 'Might be, might not be,' said Katherine. 'But there could be money in it for you, Reg, because they need a stagehand. Evening work, and not badly paid.'

'Oh, it's like Christmas come early,' said Reg, and as the cab wheels started to turn and creak he burst into song. '"*Laugh! I thought I should 'ave died, knock'd 'em in the*

Old Kent Road!'" He grinned and sat back. 'Am I 'ired?'

'It's not my decision,' said Katherine. Reg looked crestfallen.

'I don't think I've heard that song before,' I said. 'How does the rest of it go?'

'It's been all over the streets, Miss Swift, I knows it by 'eart.' And Reg launched into the song from the beginning. It was a simple melody, and soon I was singing the chorus with him.

'Connie!'

I stopped guiltily in the middle of a word. I had forgotten myself, and my face flushed. But when I dared to look at Katherine, she was smiling.

'You can sing!' she exclaimed. 'I mean, you can really sing!'

'Um, well, I had lessons, and —'

'Don't you see?'

Then I realised what she meant. 'No, Katherine, absolutely not. I am not singing on stage.'

'What?' Reg looked from one to the other of us. 'What's the plan?'

'There is no plan,' said Katherine shortly. 'Just an idea. Which won't work. Back to square one.' She folded her arms and stared out of the window, and I felt guilty again.

'If it was anything else…' I said. 'I love to sing, but I can't do it in public. Mother wanted me to do recitals, but I froze every time I tried, even in our own parlour.'

Katherine sighed, and uncrossed her arms. 'I'm sorry, I didn't mean to push. I got carried away. I'll think of something.' And she spent the rest of the journey with her elbow on the window-ledge and her chin on her hand, doing just that.

'That lad's not gonna fit on my lap,' snapped Mr Templeton.

'That's not what we had in mind,' said Katherine. 'I thought he could be a stand-in for your injured stagehand.'

'Ohhh.' Mr Templeton cocked his head on one side, considering Reg. 'He looks strong.'

'I am,' said Reg, proudly.

'Awright, seeing as I'm desperate,' said Mr Templeton. 'Come back later in clothes you can get mucky in, not that office boy get-up, and I'll put you to work.'

'Right you are, sir,' said Reg, saluting. ''Ow much is the pay, if you don't mind me asking?'

Mr Templeton raised his eyebrows. It was hard to know if he was impressed or annoyed. 'Three shillings a night, take it or leave it.'

'Three shillings a *night?'* exclaimed Reg.

Mr Templeton tutted. 'Three an' six, an' that's me final offer.'

'I'll take it!' said Reg, pumping Mr Templeton's hand.

'Settle down, young man,' said Mr Templeton, a twinkle in his eye. 'Breakages come out of that, yer know.' Reg subsided like a falling soufflé. 'Nah then.' Mr Templeton eyed Katherine and me. 'I take it this ain't a social call. What are you two after this time?'

'Information,' I said.

'I need to go on the stage for a few minutes,' said Katherine.

'Mm. Thought you weren't so keen on the stage.' Mr Templeton steepled his fingers and looked at us. 'I've given you both all the information I've got, which ain't much. I suppose you want to talk to the girls.'

'Yes please,' said Katherine.

'Ain't gonna 'appen,' he said flatly. 'They were up in arms last time you spoke to 'em. They said you'd practically accused them of keeping things back.'

'Well, they were!' I said, hotly.

'I don't doubt it,' said Mr Templeton. 'But I'm not 'aving 'em rattled. An' if they see you poking about on my stage, they'll get suspicious again. So no.' He sighed. ''Owever. There is *one* thing I can give you.'

'What?' Katherine leaned forward.

'It ain't nothing to do with Ellen,' he said, rummaging in his pocket. ''Ere you go.' And he handed Katherine a crown.

'Why are you giving me this?' she asked, looking thoroughly bewildered at the coin in her palm.

'For services rendered.' Mr Templeton leaned back in his chair. 'You did me a turn — lit'rally — and saved me bacon. That's what I'd've paid anyone else, plus a bit more for bravery cos I know it didn't come easy.'

'But I wasn't out there for more than a few minutes.'

'Nah, but the crowd seemed to like it. You ain't no Dottie Jones, but you're the right size. If only you could sing like 'er,' he said, wistfully. 'If yer could, I'd pay you the same as I paid 'er: two pound ten a week. I'm still a dummy short of an act.'

'I can't sing like Ellen Howe,' said Katherine. 'But I know a lady who can.' And she looked hard at me.

***

'I still don't see how this is going to work,' I said. 'I thought you hated being on stage.'

'I did,' said Katherine. 'I expect I shall this time, too.' She peered at a rail of costumes. 'That one looks fairly

70

modest,' she said, pulling it out and holding it up to herself. 'At least it only shows a tiny bit of ankle.'

'How long are you — *we* — planning to do this for?'

'Long enough to see where Ellen was looking the night she left, and long enough to find out what people know that they aren't telling us,' said Katherine firmly. 'I've no intention of making this my full-time career. Even if it does pay two pounds and ten shillings a week.'

'Are you swayed by the money?' I asked, before I could stop myself.

Katherine considered. 'No, but every little helps. Anyway, help me get this thing on. We haven't long till the other performers arrive. If we are a disaster, I'd rather they didn't see it.'

'Will you paint your face?' I asked.

'If we get the job,' said Katherine.

***

'Come on then,' called Mr Templeton from the stalls. 'Let the dog see the rabbit.'

'Are you ready?' Katherine whispered.

'I suppose,' I whispered back.

'Then let's go,' she said, walking onto the stage. 'I'll start with "The Boy I Love",' she called down.

'Good-oh,' shouted Mr Templeton. 'Now get on with it.'

Katherine eyed me in the wings. She opened her mouth, and I sang.

'"*I'm a young girl, and have just come over,*
Over from the country where they do things big…"'

I closed my eyes and pretended that I was in my own bedroom, singing to myself. I didn't open them again until I sang the last note. Katherine beamed at me and clapped.

71

I peeped round the wings at Mr Templeton, who was grinning fit to bust. 'Bloody 'ell,' he said. 'You two 'ud bring a tear to a glass eye. Go on, give us another. And make it a funny one this time.'

'Connie,' called Katherine, 'do you know "Where Did You Get That Hat"? And can you do it Cockney style?'

'I'll 'ave a go,' I said.

***

'No,' said Katherine. 'I'll do the dummy act, I'll wear the shirt, I'll wear the cap, but I am *not* showing my bare legs.'

'You ain't wearing a skirt,' said Mr Templeton. 'Two pound ten a week and I say that means trousers.'

'Not those breeches. They're indecent.'

'Fine,' he snapped. 'If milady wants new trousers, she can 'ave 'em. *Ron!*'

Ron appeared in the doorway. 'Yeh?'

'Yes sir, you mean. Go an buy some trousers what'll fit this young lady, pronto. Full-length — well, *her* full length. Before curtain-up, for preference.'

Ron goggled.

'NOW!' bellowed Mr Templeton. 'An' you,' he ordered Katherine, 'go and get yourself ready. I'll come down with you and explain. If you need help making up, ask someone. But do it nicely, or you'll end up with a face like a clown.'

'I wouldn't mind,' Katherine muttered. 'I don't particularly want to be recognised.'

'Well, I mind,' said Mr Templeton. 'You gotta look pretty, that's what the audience want. An' do your hair nice. Two songs in the first half, three in the second, and dummy with me next to last. If the audience like it, I'll bump you up.'

'Excuse me?' I said. 'What will you do to her?'

'Put 'er top o'the bill Monday.'

***

'What about James?' I asked, as Katherine drew a bright pink mouth on herself.

'What about Albert?' she countered. She turned to the mirror and frowned at herself. 'My mouth clashes with my hair.'

'Everything clashes with your ladyship's hair,' said one of the dancers, leaning over to grab a pot of rouge and jolting Katherine's arm.

''Ere Mabel,' said Betty the dog handler, from the next mirror, 'no need to be rude. She carn't 'elp it if she's a carrot top. And you ain't gonna improve things if you mess up 'er face. Mr T'd have your guts for garters.'

'Oh I do 'ope 'er ladyship will beg my pardon,' said Mabel curtseying. Katherine blinked as if unsure how to respond, and Mabel bounced off.

'And what about *James?*' I said.

'What about him?' Katherine's hands shook a little as she reached for a stick of green paint.

'He was furious when you were on stage as the dummy.'

'That was different,' she said. 'I felt obliged to do it. So it was a shock to both of us. Anyway, what was *he* doing last night? Dressing up and pretending.'

'That was different,' I said, 'and you know it.'

'Whoa!' A hand smacked the stick of paint away before it reached Katherine's eyelid. I looked up and saw the woman who'd opened the door to us a few days ago. 'Blue, always blue.'

'But my eyes are green,' Katherine objected.

73

'Don't matter. Still blue. That's how it's done here.' She handed Katherine a blue stick. 'Green's for witches and ghosts.'

'Thanks,' said Katherine. 'I'll remember that.'

'And your mouth should be bigger. They need to be able to see it right at the back.'

'That'll make a change,' I said.

Katherine poked me in the ribs. 'Stick to singing, Connie, and leave the repartee to me.'

'Does *she* need painting, too?' The woman looked at me speculatively and I shrank away.

'Connie's fine,' said Katherine. 'She's our secret weapon in the wings.'

'Secret weapon, eh?' The woman laughed and stuck a hand out, which I shook. 'Selina.'

'Connie.'

'Katherine.' It was like a cross between a formal visit and a pantomime.

'You the new Dottie?' Selina nodded at Katherine's dress.

'Not exactly. I'm not pretending to be twelve.'

'Good. Made me want to puke, that did.' She selected a spangled costume from the rail and strolled off.

'Dottie knew what she was about,' muttered Mabel, glaring after her.

A loud knock sounded at the door. Ron bellowed. 'Trousers for the dummy. I ain't coming in!'

Katherine got up and opened the door a fraction, returning with a pair of boy's trousers in grey flannel. 'I'd better check the fit.' She unbuttoned them and slid them on carefully. 'They're quite comfortable,' she said cautiously. 'I'll need braces though, they're loose at the waist.'

'This is one of the strangest conversations I've ever had. Seriously, Katherine, what is James going to say?'

'If James loves me when I'm pretending to be a ventriloquist's dummy, he can love me when I'm conducting an undercover investigation.' Katherine held her skirts out of the way. 'There. They'll be fine with braces.'

'I'll go and find some,' I said. 'You can finish making yourself pretty.'

I found Ellen's ragged breeches on the rail and unbuttoned the braces, but I took my time. In a short while I would be singing, if not in front of, then *to* an audience. I could feel myself growing nervous, but I couldn't let Katherine down.

If all went well, how would I explain my absence from home six nights a week?

And what on earth would happen if — no, not if, *when* James and Albert found out?

Chapter 10
Katherine

'Do you ever think that if one of us had skipped lunch that day I went shopping, we'd never have met,' said Connie the following Monday, checking her hair in the mirror. 'And if we'd never met, we wouldn't be in this mess now.'

I hoped that the scowl on her face was because she wasn't used to managing her own hairdressing.

'Come on Connie,' I said, 'there must be a tiny part of you that's enjoying it.'

I was fidgeting like a child, trying to steady my hand and apply lurid blue to my eyes.

''Ere let me, Miss Caster.' Sally, the only performer who would talk to us, took over and painted my eyelids. She was just twenty and unlike Ellen Howe, really could have been my sister if you didn't look too closely. She was small and red-headed, with bright blue eyes and a shy smile. She had watched me in rehearsals as if memorising my every step. It was disconcerting but flattering, and she certainly had a better idea of how to put make-up on.

'Pretty as a picture,' she said with a wink. 'And Miss

Fleet, don't you think she could be on the cover of a society magazine?'

Connie, elegant as ever in a simple tea-gown, bit her lip to suppress a smile. 'I'd love to see you walking along Aspidistra Avenue like that.'

Sally sniggered.

'You're as bad as James,' I said. 'I'll have you know mulberries are much more refined than aspidistras.'

But my reflection wasn't even refined enough for pot plants. I was ridiculous in a dress of bright pink and green tartan, sleeves so puffed they came up to my ears, and a décolletage that made me uncertain whether to be glad I was flat-chested or beg for something to stuff the bodice with. Aunt Alice would be scandalised. Even Father would have raised an eyebrow. Miss Robson would probably ask if I expected men to take me seriously in such attire.

'It's just as well you no longer have a job in that government office,' Connie continued. 'Because you'd be about to lose it.'

'No one will recognise me,' I said. 'And I bet none of those stuffed shirts would come here.'

'You've changed your tune. You thought it was a den of iniquity at first.'

'That was before Saturday.'

Saturday had been a triumph. The crowd had been uproarious, banging their tables with bottles and calling for more. Never in my entire life had I been the centre of attention unless I counted being reprimanded in class. I had spent twenty-six years being quiet and deferential.

'But it was so thrilling,' I explained. 'Making people laugh, making them sing along, having everyone enthralled by me.'

77

'They're not enthralled by you,' said Connie. 'They're enthralled by a shrimp called Felicity Velour and *my* singing.'

'I made them laugh.'

It was true, and I had never realised how wonderful that could feel.

The audience had lapped it up. And backstage, the girls had clapped me on the back and chatted as if we were the same species at last. I couldn't wait to do it again.

Sunday had been an agony of politeness but my dreaminess was put down to lovesickness by Aunt Alice, since James had sent just one fond but vague letter, having gone to visit his parents in the country.

But now we were back at The Merrymakers, and on stage in ten minutes.

'You've forgotten why we're here, haven't you?' said Connie, helping to arrange my skirts and smirking at the gaping neckline of my low dress. 'Do you want to borrow some powder puffs?'

'No thank you,' I said with as much dignity as I could muster. 'And I haven't forgotten about Ellen either. Something frightened her in the audience but I was too overwhelmed to look on Saturday. This evening, I'll be more focussed.'

'I can't believe how differently you're approaching this after what happened the night she disappeared.'

'It's because I've taken control,' I said. 'Come on, that's our warning bell.'

It was true. I had taken control. I would do this job on *my* terms. They'd sneer at Katherine Demeray. They'd despise Katherine Caster. Even those male members of the audience from the same circles as us would sneer. I didn't mind being laughed at, as long as I could appreciate the joke. James laughed at me constantly because he said I was prim . . . and realising that was when the penny dropped. On stage, I'd played on the things that made him laugh. I couldn't change my accent and nor could Connie, not in the time we had.

We stood in the wings and waited for my cue. Serious Katherine Demeray wasn't a snob, she was simply afraid of losing her dignity. Yet she could pretend to be someone else.

'Flowers for yer, Miss er . . . Miss,' said Reg, appearing with a large bunch of yellow roses.

'Can you put them in the dressing room,' I whispered. 'How kind of James,' I said to Connie. 'Although I wonder why he picked yellow. It's not my favourite.'

Connie opened her mouth to speak, but there was no time to talk. We were on.

This was the moment when Felicity Velour — or as James would have it, Miss Tea-Party — pranced on stage in a comic exaggeration of James's teasing view of me. I made fun of the stuck-up maiden I'd been accused of being. I became a prissy girl singing saucy words and being baffled by what was coming out of her mouth. In between songs, I danced with an imaginary suitor called Giles Milkinsop and chatted nonsense about tea-parties and lap dogs. I was the very image of the naive over-protected girl of the suburbs I had been brought up to be. The audience howled. Connie's voice during one of the songs became louder than I'd expected.

'*Don't forget…*'

I hesitated a second in my pirouette and remembered to look into the audience. It was hard to make out individual faces and I was a little afraid, but from what I could tell there were only smiles and encouragement. In the shadows someone might have been glowering but it was hard to be sure. I wondered how Ellen could have made anything out, but . . . it was that table just to the left of centre. That was where she was looking that night. I wondered what my old dancing teacher would say if she could have seen how well I danced while detecting and pretending to sing, in a dress which was slipping from my shoulders. I had a feeling she wouldn't have been proud. But I was. I pranced off to applause and cheers.

Connie touched my arm. 'Katherine —'

'There's no time,' I said, rushing past. 'You sounded lovely, but I have to change.'

I cast a quick look at the flowers, but there was no time to read the note. Connie fingered it.

'I don't mind,' I said, as I wriggled out of the dress and into my dummy costume.

I felt better about that, too. Perhaps the freedom of wearing trousers had made a difference, or perhaps what James called my terrier nature: once I'd decided what I wanted to do, nothing could stop me. But I'd do it on my terms no matter how annoying I was.

Mr Templeton carried me on stage, a dummy dressed as a lad with a ridiculous cap fringed with orange wool.

'Now then, Carrots,' he said. 'Are you going to behave today?'

I shook my head as if I was made from wood. When he spoke for me, sometimes I'd open my mouth, sometimes I wouldn't. I'd slide sideways, I'd knock my head into his. I'd pretend to yawn. The audience shrieked with laughter.

At the end, when I was 'dropped' to the stage, I danced

away on my bare feet, aiming a kick at Mr Templeton's posterior before running into the wings.

Among the shouting of 'encore' I could hear one low rumble. Was it dissent, or just a chair moving?

In the dressing room, one of the dancing girls tumbled my hair and told me what a caution I was.

'Ellenow 'ad better watch 'er back. There's a new girl in town. Mind, lovey, you need to slow down. You'll wear yourself out.' Then she skipped off.

'Katherine,' said Connie, 'have you told James about this?'

'Of course not,' I said, putting my loud dress back on for the encore.

'Then how did he know to send flowers?'

I paused and stared at her.

'What does the note say?' she said.

My hands shook as I opened it.

Go back ware you come from. Keep yore noses out. Else wotch yore back. I know ware to find you.

CHAPTER 11
Connie

I still don't know how we got through that encore. I concentrated on keeping my voice as steady as I could for our last two numbers. Katherine grinned and capered her way round the stage almost as before, but I could see a jerkiness to her movements, and underneath the paint her face was very pale. At last the curtain came down, and she sagged like the dummy she had so recently acted. I ran forward and took her arm, half-carrying her towards the dressing-room.

'Told yer you'd wear yourself out,' said one of the dancers, as she skipped by. 'You'll be no fit company for yer best boy this evening.'

'My best boy?' said Katherine, faintly.

'Yeah, the one 'oo sent you them roses.'

'Oh. No. That wasn't my best boy. I mean, I don't have a best boy —'

'Don't give me that!' The girl grinned good-humouredly. 'I saw yer looking at that one particular table, over an' over. An' if 'e ain't waiting for you outside the stage door tonight, my name ain't Molly Gandy. Well, I mean it ain't really, but you can't go on the stage with a name like Mary Stout, can yer?' She giggled, and ran ahead to the dressing room. 'You'd better 'urry or he'll 'ave scarpered!'

Katherine looked up at me, and every freckle on her face stood out against her white skin. 'I'm sorry,' she whispered. She blinked. 'I'm so sorry.'

'Don't worry,' I said, much more calmly than I felt. 'Get yourself cleaned up, and I'll take you home. I won't leave you.'

I had had to make special arrangements to accommodate our run at the Merrymakers, since Mother would never have permitted me to be out so many nights in a row. I am ashamed to say that I dictated a letter to Katherine, supposedly from a friend of mine who had moved to Brighton, inviting me for a week of sea air. I waved the letter and my train ticket at Mother, and after I had spoken several times of how much I would miss Albert, and hinted that perhaps I might stay at home after all, she practically pushed me and my trunk into the carriage. The trunk and I were now residing in a small private hotel on the outskirts of Putney, and following this morning's cheerless breakfast and a day avoiding anywhere I might be spotted, I almost missed even Mother.

I watched Katherine clean her face, wiping away the painted smile. She scuttled into the curtained area to put her day dress on. When she emerged, she jammed her hat tight on her head, and tried to tuck her hair into it. 'It's no good,' she muttered, staring at herself in the mirror and pulling the hat down. 'It's no good, this won't work.'

'No it won't.' Mabel murmured over her shoulder.

83

'Best leave sleeping dogs lie.'

'We just want to help.'

'Do yer now? Well, you might make things worse.' Mabel jammed her own hat on her curls and stalked off.

'Katherine,' I said, putting my hand on my friend's arm. 'Don't mind her. I'll get Ron to hold a cab for us, and get it to take us by an indirect route. If anyone is following, we'll lose them.'

She nodded, but I wasn't sure she'd taken in a word I said.

I found Ron in the foyer, bantering with the departing customers. Most of the performers had already changed, and some of them, especially the dancers, were now sipping a drink and being gazed at adoringly by a member of the audience. I told Ron what I wanted. 'To the front door? Course I will.' He loped outside, stuck two fingers in his mouth, and whistled.

I practically had to drag Katherine out of the deserted dressing-room. 'It'll be fine,' I reassured her. 'Keep your head down, and we'll be in the cab in less than a minute.'

The minute she appeared, a man shouted ''Ere she is! It's Fliss Velooer!' People surged forward, touching Katherine's coat, her hat, trying to take her hand.

'It's Carrots!'

'Is your 'air really that colour?'

Katherine smiled weakly and quickened her step, murmuring 'I'm very tired, sorry, I'm very tired.'

'Sign us an autograph, love!'

'Give us a kiss!'

''Ave a drink with me!'

She stopped to sign a couple of programmes which were thrust under her nose, and then, thankfully, we managed to push our way through the crowd and into the cab.

'Where to, ladies?' asked the cabman, turning.

'Sam!' I cried. 'Sam Webster!'

'The very same, ma'am.'

'To Ealing, please,' I said, loudly enough for the whole foyer to hear me.

'Fair enough!' Sam shouted, and we set off at once.

'Right,' he said, as soon as we were clear of Lambeth. 'Where *are* we going?'

'I knew you'd understand,' I said, gratefully. 'To Mulberry Avenue in Fulham, please, by as twisty a route as you like.'

'That's where your friend lives, isn't it?'

'That's right.'

He was silent for a moment. 'I won't ask why you two ladies 'ave been frequenting a music hall in Lambeth, because you won't give me a straight answer if I do.'

'You wouldn't believe me if I did,' I replied, sinking back into the padded seat. We jolted over a stone in the road, and Katherine tensed.

'Ssh,' I said, feeling for her hand and squeezing it. 'You're safe. We're with Sam, and he'll take us home. Take you home, I mean.'

'Oh, Connie —'

'I'll be fine,' I said, though I felt far from it. 'I'll make sure my door's locked at the hotel.' I looked at Katherine. 'What are we going to do?'

A look of pain crossed her face. 'I don't know,' she whispered. 'I'm too scared to think straight.'

That was the worst part of it all. Katherine always knew what to do. 'Let's meet tomorrow,' I said.

'I can't,' she muttered. 'Dr Farquhar's expecting me at the surgery.'

I sighed. 'We'll work something out,' I said. I had no idea how, or what.

After what seemed a very long time, we drew up outside Katherine's house. 'I'll watch you go in,' I said.

I felt the tremor in her hand as I let it go. 'Thank you,' she said.

I held my breath as she scurried across the pavement and climbed the steps. Although her key was ready, she appeared to fumble it into the lock. Finally the door swung shut behind her.

I exhaled. Katherine was safe, at least for tonight. I closed my eyes in relief.

In that moment the cab door was wrenched open and someone got in. I groped for the other door handle and opened my mouth to scream.

'No you don't,' said a furious voice, and a hand clamped over my mouth. 'Where the *hell* have you been?'

I opened my eyes. Though it was dark, I could just make out the features of Albert Lamont, looking angrier than I had ever seen him.

***

'Get out, Connie. Please.'

Albert paid Sam's fare, with a generous tip, and the cab drove into the night.

'Tredwell is waiting.' He did not take my arm, and I did not dare ask. We walked side by side, but not close.

'How did you —'

'We'll talk inside.' He held the door open for me and helped me in, but as if it were a duty, not a pleasure. I longed to take his hand, but the thought of him snatching it

86

away made me blink back tears.

We drove for some time before he spoke. 'It wasn't difficult,' he said, staring straight ahead. 'I called at your house, and your mother sent me packing, informing me that you had gone to stay with a friend for the week.' The ice-blue glare again. 'She seemed rather pleased that you hadn't bothered to tell me.'

'I'm sorry, I didn't think —'

'Then I called at Katherine's, and Aunt Alice very kindly told me that I'd find her at your house.' He looked away. 'I'm not stupid.'

'I'm really sorry, Albert, I —'

'Whatever you're about to say, don't lie. What have you been doing?'

I looked up from my twisting hands then, into his face, and if I had seen any kindness there, I would have poured it all out. But all I could see was anger; a set, hard mouth and eyes that bored into me.

'I can't tell you.'

'What do you mean?' I had thought his eyes were piercing before, but now I couldn't look at him.

And yet, somehow, I stood my ground. 'I'm not going to tell you. It isn't any business of yours.'

'It isn't my business?' He almost shouted the words. 'My cousin and — you — have been doing God knows what, and it's nothing to do with me?'

'I'm not your cousin.' I raised my voice. 'Stop the carriage please, Tredwell.'

'*No.*' He seized my wrist and I yelped. 'Sorry,' he muttered, releasing it immediately. 'But you aren't leaving this carriage until you tell me the truth.'

'Oh yes I am,' I said, hammering on the panel between

ourselves and Tredwell. 'You have no right to — to shadow either me or your cousin, who is my dearest friend, and you have no right to demand to know our business.'

He closed his eyes and leaned against the seat, and I waited for him to smile, to admit that he had been wrong, to take my hand and apologise. But when Albert opened his eyes there was no smile, no acknowledgement.

'Then it's over.'

'What — what —' I stammered.

He did not look angry now, not at all, just desperately sad. 'How can I marry a woman I can't trust? How could I, when you've lied to me —'

'I haven't lied to you —'

'You didn't tell me the truth, and you won't tell me now.' He dashed a hand across his eyes. 'I love you, and you've thrown it back at me.'

'I haven't done anything wrong!' I cried. Tears were streaming down my face, but I didn't care. 'I haven't, I promise!'

'Then why won't you tell me?' Albert's voice cracked on the last word, and I laid my head on his chest and sobbed my heart out. After a few moments I felt his arms around me, and he sighed as he held me close. 'Where do I need to take you?'

'I have a room at the Rosemere, in Putney. My trunk is there.'

'Good Lord.' He was silent for a few moments. 'Tredwell!'

'Sir?' came through the panel.

'To the Rosemere in Putney, please.'

'Sorry, sir. The horses won't take much more.'

Albert and I looked at each other. 'I can't go home,' I

said, firmly.

'Then we'll go to *my* home,' he said.

***

It was past midnight when the carriage finally drew up at the Lamont family residence.

'The servants will be in bed,' whispered Albert. 'They know not to wait up.'

'But — what if someone sees me?' I asked, my heart sinking.

'I'll explain,' said Albert. 'There's no way you could get a cab to Putney now.'

Tredwell dropped us outside the front door, and drove round to the stable. Albert let us in. 'I'll put you in a guest room near mine,' he whispered. 'I'll try and smuggle you out in the morning.'

We crept up the thickly-carpeted stairs, and along a wide corridor. 'That's my room,' said Albert, pointing at a door which looked exactly like all the others we had passed. 'You can have this one.' He opened another identical door and switched on the light, revealing a pretty, chintzy room, with a sofa at the foot of the bed. 'I'll go and find you, um, a nightshirt or something.'

'Thank you.'

He returned within two minutes, a blue-and-white striped nightshirt over his arm. 'I brought a brush. I thought you might need one.'

'I don't think I've ever been so glad to see a hairbrush,' I said, removing my hat.

Albert regarded the hotchpotch of pins with curiosity. 'It — doesn't look very comfortable,' he ventured.

'It isn't,' I said, easing out the spikiest hairpins.

'Why don't you sit down with me,' he said, patting the

seat next to him, 'and brush it out?'

I was too tired to argue, and somehow, as I passed Albert my hairpins and he loosened his tie, it seemed perfectly normal to tell him what we had been doing. He listened, and didn't interrupt, and he wasn't angry. After a while the electric light was too harsh and bright, and Albert opened the curtains so that we could talk by moonlight instead. I managed to plait my hair, and tie it with Albert's shoelace, and the last thing I remember was Albert complaining that my hair was tickling him, before I woke up bathed in morning light, stiff and chilly, curled on the sofa in the crook of Albert's arm.

CHAPTER 12
Katherine

I stood at the window of my little office at Dr Farquhar's, peering at the street. I wasn't getting much done. Quite apart from the confusion of the doctor's memoirs, which had reached a period in his life so apparently exciting that it was incoherent, I couldn't focus and kept making mistakes. The sun shone on the paper and my typewriter in great golden stripes. The air was clear today, but if it carried on as hot, it would be dense, opaque and unbreathable by tomorrow. Summer or no, fires had to be lit to run London, and smoke blurred the blue skies. It would be lovely to be outside while it was still pleasant.

But my mind churned. I had had no word from Connie and she had expressly said not to contact her first. I had a feeling she hadn't told me everything, and worried that she had been so foolhardy as to stay in a hotel alone, when she could have stayed with me. I would have thought twice about doing such a thing. I could only hope she was safe and indeed that I was safe too. I hadn't heard from James either, and hoped that when he returned I would not snap at him out of sheer anxiety. Albert had been distracted when I'd last seen him, too. There were far too many secrets at the moment.

I sat down, pulled a crumpled sheet of bad typing from the bin and started to write on the reverse. Ellen was missing. Was she hiding or had she been taken? The actions of the person who'd sent the flowers could imply either, but somehow it seemed more likely that she was still at large and someone wanted to get to her before we did. A man. Ellen hadn't struck me as the sort who is nervous of men. It had been a man who'd glowered in the shadows, the handwriting on the note was surely a man's and flowers are a man's trick.

I sketched the roses and thought how ironic it was that my first bouquet was from an ill-wisher, not a lover. And in the middle of it all was Ellen. A fully grown woman who dressed like a girl. A woman from the country. A skilled and successful performer who had London, or at least, some elements of it, at her feet. I felt the same thrill I had last night, and wondered how she could bear to give it up. How big must the threat to her be? Worse still, what alternative means of income did she have?

Flowers…

There was a knock on the door and Mallory popped his head round.

'Wire for you, Miss Demeray.'

'Thank you.'

I took it from him, trying to hide the trembling of my hand. What if I really was being followed?

But it was from Connie. *Tulips didn't beat us last year STOP Romano's lunch at one QUERY More than safe STOP.*

I was still puzzling when there was another knock at the door, but it stayed shut. I paused, but anyone entering the building would have to get past Mallory.

'Come in.'

The door opened but still no one entered. I looked round for something to arm myself with. All I had was a wastepaper bin and typewriter. One would be useless, the other lethal.

A book flew across the room and landed on my desk. It was entitled *Self-Defence for Suburban Ladies*.

'I was going to bring flowers.' James entered the room, his face almost as sober as it had been when I last saw him, but with half a hopeful smile. 'But I'd probably buy the wrong colour and you'd misinterpret what I was trying to say.'

'How should I interpret a book on self-defence? Do you actually want me to fight off your advances?'

Before James could answer, the door opened again and Dr Farquhar came in.

'Miss Demeray, I have to say I've noticed you looking more than a little weary and stressed lately. I see you have a caller, and I prescribe an afternoon off while the weather is so good. I'll see you on Thursday.'

I gathered my things, stuffing the scribbled notes into my bag. James picked up the book and we stepped out into the sun. He hailed a cab. 'I thought we'd take a walk in St James's Park,' he said. 'Would that suit you?' He said nothing else. When we arrived, he offered his elbow for me to hold.

We walked in silence until I said 'I hope you had a lovely time in the country with your family.'

'Oh,' he said, as if he'd forgotten their existence. 'They

send their regards.'

I had never met his parents. I wondered what he'd told them about me. Perhaps nothing.

Finally he stopped at a bench. No-one was near.

'Let's stop here.' He made no attempt to sit close, and stared down the path in silence. I rose.

'I think I'll go home,' I said. 'The doctor is right. I'm very tired.' I had so wanted to ask his advice, but he didn't care enough for it to matter any more.

'No!' His urgency startled me and I sat again.

'Katherine,' he said. 'I want to explain why I asked you about Henry.'

'I thought you believed me.'

'I do. Albert said one evening that there had been an understanding between the two of you. I'm sorry I asked the way I did. I'd like us to be friends.'

Friends.

I cleared my throat. 'May I ask if you try to kiss all your friends in cabs?' It came out wrong. I hadn't meant to sound waspish and cold.

'Only the ones who are short stubborn red-heads.' Was that a smile?

'What have you found out about Ellen?' he said. He had moved a little closer and his foot touched mine.

'What makes you think we're still looking?'

'You're tired and worried. I'm not blind. What have you been doing? I had an incoherent wire from Albert, and you look like death. I wish you'd waited till I was back, but you won't give me the right to look after you. And stop bristling.'

'I'm not.'

'You are. Anyway, I wrote to explain why I'd gone to

the country, and that it was about Ellen, and you still didn't wait, did you?'

I stared.

'I received one letter saying you were visiting your parents. I thought you'd just . . . left. Tell me. Tell me now.'

James shook his head. 'I'm sorry,' he said. 'I don't know what happened, I asked someone at home to post the letter for me. I should have done it myself. Forgive me.'

I felt myself relax a little. 'Perhaps we both jumped to conclusions. Tell me what it said.'

'You remember Mr and Mrs Johns, the couple at Paddington with the little boy?'

'Yes.'

'They knew her, they knew Ellen. When they were reunited with their daughter, Mrs Johns said to her "We were so afraid you'd disappear like Helen Henderson." I didn't think anything of it. They called her 'Elen 'Enderson. And then the daughter said "I thought I saw 'Elen on a poster, only she was called something else so it couldn't have been. And she had black hair, like 'Elen's little girl."'

'I don't understand.'

'Helen Henderson ran away to London. Her family didn't see her for several years. Then she came home with a baby. She was in a terrible state, they said, but she couldn't settle. After a while, she returned to London. She told them not to look for her and hasn't been back since. She sends money, but that's all. I took the Johns family home and saw the little girl. If that wasn't Ellen Howe's child, I'm a ballerina.'

I tried to absorb this. It still didn't explain why she'd

disappeared now or why she dressed as a child.

James sighed. 'Have you forgiven me enough to tell me what you've been up to, and why you look so scared?'

Too many secrets. I took a deep breath and hoped his sense of humour was still under the surface.

'You weren't there to advise, so we, *I* decided we'd have to go back to the Merrymakers when it was in full swing.'

'Please don't tell me —'

It took me ten minutes to explain my performances and Connie's singing. So many conflicting expressions crossed James's face I thought he'd explode.

'Not 'arf good too, weren't yer, Miss D?' Reg had sneaked up on us.

'Shouldn't you be at work?' I admonished.

'I'm a messenger boy ain't I?' said Reg, 'and I've got a message to take to the Ministry. It's a nice day, so I thought I'd go the long way round. Just as well, cos now I've bumped into you and can give my report.'

'Report?' said James.

'I'd better be quick. But the thing is, on the way 'ome I had a feeling I was followed but if I was, I give 'em the slip. I reckon we was all being watched last night.'

James groaned, 'Oh Katherine, what have you not told me this time?'

Swallowing, I explained about the flowers and the note. The sense of menace.

'And you wonder why I've brought you a book instead of roses,' he said. 'I thought maybe you'd learn to protect yourself, if you won't let anyone else do it. It seemed like a useful present. I just planned that you'd learn the techniques *before* the next crisis.'

96

'Any'ow,' said Reg, 'gotta go. I can't wait for this evening's performance. She's a caution, Mr King. You gotta see her.'

He bounced off down the lane and James and I sat in silence.

'Dammit, Katherine,' he said. 'I don't know whether to lock you up, kiss you or strangle you.'

'I know which I'd prefer.'

'I suppose you're annoyed that I didn't bring flowers. Well, I'm not. I'd be better buying you a suit of armour. Or a one-way ticket to Tunbridge Wells.'

Flowers. A rich man's gift. Expensive. The man who'd written the ill-spelt, scruffy note was unlikely to be able to afford flowers that weren't the wilted remnants of a florist's unsold stock. So were those yellow roses stolen? How else could he have got them while they were fresh?

CHAPTER 13
Connie

Albert was still asleep, and I didn't want to disturb him; that would start the day, and end the night. I studied the way his hair, so neat in the daytime, fell forward over his forehead, and the fresh dark stubble on his jaw. I watched his chest rise and fall beneath the open collar of his shirt. And I wished we could stay like that for ever, because I had no idea what would happen next.

A slight movement from Albert's arm told me that he was waking; then a sudden halt, as if he was registering where he was. I waited for his eyes to open, and braced myself for whatever expression they might hold — surprise? horror? But they stayed closed.

'Tell me,' he said. 'If I open my eyes, will you definitely still be here?'

'Yes,' I whispered, stroking his cheek and marvelling at the roughness where the stubble began.

'That's good.' He smiled. 'I thought I dreamt the whole thing. About you, and the music hall, and — everything.'

'It's all real,' I said, and Albert's eyes opened, his

pupils shrinking at the light in the room. 'It's all real.'

***

Albert wriggled his watch from his waistcoat pocket. 'It's half past seven. I have a meeting at ten.' He propped himself on his elbow and played with the end of my plait.

'Oh.' I imagined myself either shut up in this room for the morning or smuggled out into the street.

'I'd like you to come, but I must speak to Father first.'

'Wha —?' I stared at him. 'You're going to tell your father I'm here?'

Albert grinned. 'I need to consult him on a couple of matters. And I have something to ask you, too. But I can do that after breakfast. I'll ring for a tray.'

I clutched his arm. 'But they'll see —'

Albert loosened my grip. 'I'll ring from my room, Connie. Don't worry, you're quite safe.' But the dancing light in his eyes made me suspect that I very possibly wasn't.

He arrived with the tray ten minutes later. 'Room service, madam,' he announced, manoeuvring round the door cautiously. 'I have no idea how Dinsdale makes it look so easy.' He caught sight of my hair, which I had spent the intervening time pinning up as neatly as I could, and his face fell a little. 'You look tidy, Connie.'

'I don't feel it.' And I didn't. My dress was crumpled, and I longed for a good soak in a bath. I had inspected myself closely in the mirror while doing my hair, and I looked as if another eight hours' sleep would not go amiss. But the main surprise to me was that I looked as much like myself as I did. I had almost expected to see a different person looking back from the glass.

'You'll feel better when you've eaten.' He put the tray

99

on the low table, sat beside me, and kissed me, and suddenly I felt much, much better.

***

Albert was as smart as ever by the time he went to his father's study. I passed the time in trying to smooth out my dress, re-pinning my hair in an attempt to make it less like a bird's nest, and staring at the pages of a volume of sentimental poems, which had presumably been banished to the guest room since no one else wanted to read them. How long would Albert be gone? What was he talking about with his father? Where were we going afterwards, and why did Albert want me to come? The thought that Albert might have work or business commitments had never once occurred to me, and I reflected guiltily on my own lack of any kind of useful employment. I didn't volunteer for any charities or missions; I didn't knit socks for soldiers; I didn't even help with the rummage sales at our church, beyond donating old clothes.

I jumped when the door opened, and the book of poems slid from my lap. 'Sorry,' said Albert. 'I didn't mean to startle you.' He was smiling.

'Is everything all right?' I asked.

'So far, yes,' he said. 'But I haven't got to the important bit yet.'

'What's that?' The meeting, I supposed. I imagined a room full of elderly men in brocade waistcoats, and Albert doing — well, whatever it was that Albert did, while I fidgeted in a waiting room.

The smile faded from his face as he approached the sofa. 'Connie, I, um…' He scratched his ear. 'This is harder than I thought.'

My heart fell like a stone. 'Albert, what is it?'

100

He straightened his necktie as if it were a noose, not looking at me. 'I — oh damn it.' Suddenly he plopped down on the sofa and took my hand. 'Connie, please will you marry me?'

I stared at him in utter amazement. I tried to speak, but my mouth had lost the ability to form words.

'It was that stupid row in the cab, it made me realise I couldn't bear the thought of losing you. When I thought — oh never mind. I was meant to kneel down, wasn't I, and I completely forgot.'

'It doesn't matter,' I said, absently. I could barely take it in. Such an overwhelming thing, in five little words. The room lurched, and I grabbed the arm of the sofa to steady myself. Albert's hold on my hand tightened, and I looked up at him, at his dear, worried, wonderful face.

'Yes,' I whispered, and managed to smile. 'Yes!' I threw my arms around his neck, and we landed in a giggling heap on the sofa.

***

'Where are we going?'

'Coutts' Bank,' said Albert, as Tredwell eased the horses to a stop. 'And here we are.' He laughed at my mystified face. 'Connie, you look so puzzled,' he said, as he handed me down the steps.

'That's because I am,' I said. Perhaps I was pessimistic, but having a meeting at the bank did not sound positive. Then again, if it were so bad, Albert wouldn't have asked me to come.

'I thought it was important that you know the truth, before we proceed any further,' he said, and as he led me through the ornate double doors my feet seemed to grow heavier.

Did I want to know the truth? Mother's words were ringing in my head now. 'He's a youngest son, Constance. He probably has scarcely tuppence to call his own,' she had said, her lip curling. 'But if you want to live in genteel poverty, that is your affair.'

'Mr Lamont!' A beaming official hurried forward. 'How nice to see you! And this is…?' He inclined his head towards me, eyebrows raised.

'This is Miss Swift,' said Albert. 'I know I can count on your discretion.'

'Oh, *absolutely*. Mr Anstruther is ready for you, if you will just step this way.'

'Excellent.' We followed our greeter down a thickly-carpeted corridor, its walls lined with paintings, the utter opposite of the bare, peeling corridors of the music hall.

'Mr Lamont, good morning.' Mr Anstruther, a slight, sandy-haired man with a Scots burr, was standing behind his desk in readiness for us.

'Good morning, Anstruther.' Albert set a chair for me, then took a seat. 'Allow me to introduce Miss Swift.'

The banker's eyes swivelled in my direction and he held out a hand, murmuring, 'Delighted.' I could tell that I wasn't really the focus of his attention, though.

'I won't keep you too long,' said Albert, 'but I'd like to know your present thoughts on gold bullion. I have an opinion, and I'm curious to learn if you agree.'

'That *is* interesting,' said Mr Anstruther, a gleam in his eye, and they conversed rapidly on flow and purity, reserves, bandying numbers about till I felt giddy. I realised that I was staring, and fixed my gaze firmly on my clasped hands. They moved on to steel, and copper, and it was possibly the most incomprehensible ten minutes of my life.

'So we agree,' said Albert. 'Two to gold bullion, one and a half to steel, both out of the bonds, and wait and see on copper. To be monitored, of course.'

'Of course,' Mr Anstruther echoed, scribbling with a gold fountain pen. 'And your managed holdings?'

'The same, please.'

'I'll see it is done immediately.' Mr Anstruther drew a firm line beneath his note. 'Will there be anything else today, sir?'

'Just one thing. Could you furnish me with a statement of account, please?'

Mr Anstruther's eyes narrowed a little. 'For all holdings, or your personal holdings?'

Albert smiled at me. 'Just my personal holdings, if you don't mind.'

'It will be a pleasure. Excuse me one moment.' Mr Anstruther rose and took down a large ledger, opening it to the last inscribed page. Drawing a sheet of headed notepaper towards him, he wrote down a column of numbers, then consulted what looked like a price list, and conjured a new, much larger set of numbers in a different column, which he added. 'I get it to that,' he said, handing the paper to Albert.

Albert glanced at the paper. 'Yes, that seems about right. Do wire me if there's any hold-up with the transfers, won't you?' He folded the paper, handed it to me, and rose.

'But of course,' said Mr Anstruther. 'Lovely to meet you, Miss Swift. Would you like someone to show you out?'

'I think we'll manage,' said Albert, opening the door for me.

'You can look, you know,' he said, as we walked down the corridor. I was glad that we were unescorted this time; I was full of questions.

'But I thought —' My words trailed off as he turned to me, and we stopped.

'You thought what?'

I tried to find a way to phrase it without sounding mercenary. 'I, um, I…'

Albert let me dangle for a second or two. 'You thought I was the broke younger son.' He grinned. 'Well, I am the youngest in the family.' He nodded at the paper in my hand. 'I thought you'd be curious.'

'I am, but…'

'I wanted you to know that my circumstances are reasonable.'

Slowly I unfolded first one, then the other fold of the paper. My eyes scanned the columns, until I arrived at the figure on the bottom right. Then I gasped.

'That can't be —'

'It is. You saw Anstruther work it out before your very eyes.'

'I know, but that isn't reasonable. That's ridiculous.'

'I suppose it is, when you aren't used to it. Would you like a cup of tea?'

'I certainly would,' I said, taking Albert's arm and passing the paper back to him. 'But only if you're quite sure you can afford it.'

***

Due to my need to lay low, we secured a room at a nearby hotel, where an obsequious waiter served us elevenses. 'Tell me,' I said, laying my hand on his.

Albert gazed across at me. 'I shall. But this is on the

understanding that it goes no further. Not without my consent.'

'I promise.'

'It began when I was twenty,' said Albert, selecting a biscuit. 'Father informed me that when I came of age a few months later he would settle a small private income on me, as he had with my elder siblings. It would be mine to do as I wished with, and I was free to live in the family home for his lifetime, at least. But he warned me that beyond that, he could offer no further financial support. Some of his investments had failed, and he was determined that Maurice, my eldest brother, would have enough money to be able to keep the house going and live comfortably.'

'Go on.'

'As you may have noticed, I like to be well-dressed. I had already been roasted for exceeding my allowance, and so I determined that I would have to do the best I could with the money I had. That's when I started studying investments. My capital was in Consols — three percenters — and I thought I could do better. So I took a small portion of it, and tried. It worked, and gradually I increased the proportion of money I invested elsewhere, until now, at twenty-five, things are as you see.'

'But why doesn't anyone know?'

'I've seen the effect that money has on people.' Albert smiled sadly. 'I mean on people who think you have some. I've seen the letters Father gets, asking for subscriptions and donations to this and that, and loans to strangers with wonderful money-making schemes. I've seen the mothers thrusting their simpering daughters at Maurice, and speculating behind their hands about his wealth, my father's health, and the value of our home.' He looked into my eyes. 'So I decided to keep it a private matter. I donate anonymously to causes I believe in, and allow myself a few luxuries, like the carriage and Tredwell.' He grinned. 'Ironically, I now manage three-quarters of Father's money for him. He asked if I'd consider taking on a quarter of it when I was twenty-two, and we went from there.'

'I see.' Then a horrible thought came to me, and I barely kept from groaning. 'Oh, if Mother found out! The name-dropping, and the trousseau, and the wedding arrangements . . . it doesn't bear thinking about!'

'Exactly.' Albert moved to sit beside me, and took my hand. 'I didn't invite you here to brag, Connie, but I wanted to reassure you that you wouldn't have to worry about money. I wanted to reassure you that you would be safe.' He kissed me, very gently. 'And speaking of safe, we should probably get in touch with K.'

I felt shockingly guilty for not having thought of her. 'You're right, of course. I'll wire her at Dr Farquhar's, and offer lunch.' I paused. 'Would you mind if — we didn't tell anyone just yet? We haven't asked my father, and — there's finding Ellen, too.'

'Yes,' Albert said, contemplatively. 'I'd forgotten that I'm marrying a star of the stage.'

'That will be over soon,' I said. 'It has to be. We have to find her.'

'I know,' said Albert. 'And I won't sweep you off your feet till the case is resolved. But in the meantime, we need a plan.'

CHAPTER 14
Katherine

Connie trembled all the way through a lunch she hardly touched. Her cheeks were pink and I wondered if she had a fever.

'I can tell Mr Templeton you're not well,' I said. 'Maybe Betty will help out with the singing.'

'I couldn't be better,' said Connie, her eyes glazing over as she looked into the middle distance, and the waiter removed her uneaten food. I was afraid she'd faint. 'Besides,' she continued, 'Betty doesn't know the lyrics you wrote.'

'K wrote lyrics?' exclaimed Albert, 'I mean, I'm sure they're very erudite, but a music hall audience expect a little more —'

'Oh I don't think erudite is the word I'd use,' said Connie, and giggled. She and Albert stared into each other's eyes and fell silent.

James nudged me and rose.

'If you'll excuse us, Katherine and I have something to do.'

Connie giggled.

'Are you sure you're quite well?' I said.

'I'm very well indeed,' she answered and touched Albert's little finger with her own under the shadow of her wine glass. 'We'll see you at the theatre at half past six.'

She said the word 'theatre' in low serious tones and started to giggle again.

James steered me outside, hailed a cab and helped me in. 'What in earth is wrong with those two?' he said as he took his seat. 'I've known Albert since I was eight and I've never seen him look that unfocused without a lot more beer being involved. And as for Connie, she looked ready to smother him in kisses at a moment's notice.'

'Perhaps he gave her a sentimental present. It tends to bring out the romantic in people.'

'Well, I've given you a book, and I promise that in a short while you'll be in my arms and clasped to my chest whether you like it or not.'

'Nonsense,' I said. 'Did I hear you give the driver an address in Kensington? I'm not sure any of the museums can help us find Ellen. I don't think it's that kind of problem, do you?'

'I'm taking you to my aunt's house. Stop gaping. Connie's mother would tell you that a lady doesn't show surprise. Aunt Penelope is back from India. Failed engagement. Not sure if it was the man or the climate or the other women. She's a bit of a free spirit. More to the point, she has a garden.'

'But James —'

'Stop panicking. It's not a social call. I need her there for propriety, but in point of fact, I could make passionate love to you in the drawing room and she wouldn't care.'

I struggled for a reply.

'Don't panic, that's not what I'm planning. It's not the drawing room we need, but the garden.'

'You can't — I can't — we can't — not in the garden!' I spluttered.

He grinned, 'So you might let me in the drawing room?'

The images flooding my head made my face grow hot.

'Maybe after you've solved your case,' he went on, 'since it clearly appeals. Ah, here we are. Have you got your book?' We disembarked outside a tall, elegant house.

'Right,' he said, 'I know you're an independent woman and I respect that, but I'm not letting you go back to that music hall without preparation.'

'We get time to rehearse.'

'I don't mean rehearsals, I mean self-defence. My Japanese friend has taught me a few skills, and I plan to pass them on to you. Roll your sleeves up, Katherine. You're not leaving till you can beat me three times in a row.'

***

Even Connie came out of her reverie to stare, her well-bred neutral expression dissolved by the sight of me, red faced and hair in a plait, rushing into the dressing room.

The other girls giggled. ''Ere someone's had a nice time in the park. Charlie's dead and looking green round the gills.'

I glanced down. The grass-stained edge of my petticoat was peeping out from under my skirt.

'It's not what —' I stopped. Maybe it would do my backstage reputation good. As long as they never came across Aunt Alice and told her.

I stripped to my underwear and applied powder everywhere. 'Ju-jitsu,' I whispered to Connie.

'Bless you.'

'No, it's a sort of fighting. James has had me wrestling with him all afternoon. In the end, I could sit on his chest.'

Connie blinked. Betty, who'd leaned over to get some rouge, sniggered.

'Sure it was his chest?'

Unsure what she meant, I ignored her and started to brush my hair. Perhaps I'd leave it down. James had pulled out all my hairpins as I tried to pin *him* down, and I had only found half of them. I paused, remembering his arms holding me close, his hands in my hair, his face smiling into mine, close enough to kiss.

'Katherine, wake up.'

I pulled myself together and finding a tortoiseshell comb on the table, fastened my hair with that. Tonight's dress was in emerald green and orange stripes. The orange was so vibrant it made my hair look dull in comparison. The petticoat underneath was pink.

'My goodness,' said Connie. 'I am so glad I don't have to go on stage looking such a fright. Heaven knows what Albert would say.'

'But it's all right to let James see me like this?' Suddenly I felt nervous. What if he was shocked? What if he was embarrassed? What if he thought I was a loose woman?

'Flars for yer, Miss Caster.'

One of the stagehands shoved a dripping bundle of pink peonies through the doorway. They weren't as pristine as the roses, but still pretty. There was no note.

'Yellow roses mean dying love, or infidelity,'

110

whispered Connie. 'Peonies mean bad luck.' She looked from the flowers to me, and I saw fear in her eyes.

I swallowed and looked into the mirror at the stranger in stage paint, and then at Connie's anxious face. I had to pull myself together. Ellen was in danger, and this place must hold the key. I needed to put a smile back on Connie's face.

'So what have you and Albert been up to?'

She sighed, but the smile came back.

'She ain't the one who's been rolling in the grass,' said Betty, grabbing a stick of greasepaint. 'And you're supposed to be a lady. But ladies can do what they like and get away with it, can't they? Not like us what have to earn a living.'

I would have retorted but Connie shook her head. Our warning bell had rung,

'Were you really rolling in the grass with James?' she muttered, in the wings.

'Connie! Of course I wasn't. At least only when I pulled him off balance. I mean . . . anyway, there he is, in the audience with Albert.'

They were sitting at one of the tables, sharing a bottle of wine. Albert, I suspected, was wincing at its quality. At least they'd had time to put on proper evening dress. Unaccompanied women were circling, looking for somewhere to sit. Albert ran his finger round his collar and looked at the ceiling. James was talking to them. One looked as if she was about to sit on his knee. 'Places please,' called the stage manager. Connie fussed with her hair.

'No one's going to see you,' I whispered. 'I'm the one he'll be, I mean they'll be looking at.'

111

'Shh, your cue's coming up.'

'Break a leg, Miss Caster,' whispered Sally, who'd crept up to watch. 'Why are you shivering? You'll be wonderful.'

I swallowed. The glowering man might be somewhere in the auditorium. There were more than a few well-dressed men out there, but why would a rich man, what Mr Templeton would call a gent, bother about Little Dottie Jones? And I was sure the man in the shadows was the rougher sort — then again, only a fairly rich man could buy flowers unless —

'Go on!' Connie gave me a small push.

It's all pretend, it's all pretend. This is not Katherine Demeray, spinster of the parish, it's Felicity Velour, spinster of an entirely different parish.

I minced across the stage with my nose in the air and mimed to Connie's lovely voice:

> *I'm a lady you know*
> *A real proper miss*
> *I told him I couldn't*
> *Give him a kiss*
> *I thought he'd come back*
> *And try it once more*
> *But it seems he's lost interest*
> *In F'licity Velour.*
> *All that I want*
> *Is a love that will last*
> *And all that I do*
> *Is fall flat on my —*
> *Grass! Grass! He's looking for greener grass*
> *How I wish I'd let him make a tiny pass!*
> *Ladies, don't forget*

When they offer a little pet
If you say no, before you know
They'll be looking for greener grass.

I glanced into the audience and made the mistake of looking at Albert first. Shadowed as it was, it was hard to miss the utter astonishment in his face. James had a strange woman half-looking over the back of his chair, but he was grinning and raised a glass to me. *He'll never let me forget this.*

I finished the song and moved into a little repartee, exaggerating my natural accent and staring straight at James.

'Oh ladies, I do like a strong man, don't you? But I also like one who's a *pushover*. You can do *so* much more with them.'

What had just come out of my mouth? I nodded to the orchestra and the music started for my next song. It felt like a year before I left the stage. The laughs and cheers were not enough to obliterate the expression on James's face. No wonder he didn't think to buy me flowers. He must think I was a buffoon.

'Albert looked rather put out,' said Connie.

'The last time he saw me on stage I was an angel in a nativity play.'

'I'm not sure if that was it. James didn't seem to mind that woman pestering him. Albert had better keep ignoring the other one.'

'Mmm.'

'Was he out there?'

My mind was blank of all but embarrassment, and it would shortly get worse. After Betty and Buster and a dance by the girls, Carrots would be disobeying his puppet master. James would either drop dead or kill Mr Templeton or more likely, run away with the trollop.

'The man. The one you noticed last time.'

'Oh. I'm not sure.'

'Katherine, *pay attention*.'

In the dressing room I sped to change costumes, whipping off Felicity's hideous dress and petticoat and stripping to my corset and drawers.

'Gotta 'and it to yer,' said Mabel, the last one to leave for the stage. 'You're not too proud to make a fool of yerself.' Her smile was almost friendly.

I pulled Carrots's shirt and trousers on, and popped the fringed cap over my hair.

'That's odd,' said Connie. We were alone in the room. The dancers were lined up in the wings, and the acrobats had left for their next music hall.

'What is?'

'There wasn't a note with the flowers, was there?'

'No.'

'There's one now. In fact, there are two. Who was the last one addressed to?'

I realised I hadn't looked properly at the envelope. I'd assumed the note was for me, as the flowers had been handed to me. 'I think it said *To the singer*.'

'Well, that one says *To the singer* and thinking about it, that's not you. It's me,' said Connie. 'The other is definitely addressed to Miss Caster, but it's in different writing.'

We had a few minutes until Betty returned. I opened the envelopes.

The one to *The singer* said: *I told you. Yore not wonted.*

114

Go back ware you come from. Or else.

The other letter said: *Deer Miss Caster. Pleese stop looking for me. You put me in mor danger. Ellen Howe.*

Connie and I looked at each other. Under my boy's shirt my heart beat faster, and the music beyond the dressing room was drowned out by the thudding in my head.

'What should we do?' whispered Connie.

'We can't stop,' I said. 'We must find her before he does. The flower man. He means her harm. We need to find her, or find him.'

'But where? There are hundreds of florists.'

'But only one place a poor man can get flowers easily at the end of the day,' I said. 'Covent Garden.'

Connie groaned. 'As if Lambeth wasn't bad enough. Albert is never going to agree.'

'It's not his decision, is it?' I said. 'Is it?'

CHAPTER 15
Connie

'Come on, Katherine.' She was sitting at a dressing table, her eyes unfocused, with a pot of cold cream in one hand and a cloth in the other. 'They'll be waiting.'

'That's what worries me.' She dabbed at one blue eyelid. 'James looked . . . I don't know.'

'Albert didn't look exactly pleased,' I said. I looked at Ellen's note again to distract myself. The same pink envelope, the same rounded writing. *No postmark*. 'This has been hand-delivered. She's been here, Katherine.'

'Yes.' She sounded weary, sad, almost defeated. 'I know.' Suddenly she dipped the cloth into the pot and began to scrub at herself more energetically. 'You're right. We need to get moving.'

***

Albert and James were waiting for us in the corridor when we finally emerged. 'Well, that was a show,' said James, grinning.

'Yes, it was,' said Katherine. 'Did you enjoy it?'

'It was fascinating,' he replied.

Albert offered me an arm, his face neutral. 'Did you see anything?' I asked. I wanted to focus on something other than the expression I had seen on his face while I was singing.

'We'll talk later,' he said. 'Come along.'

And yet, a few moments later as the horses got up speed, we found ourselves looking at each other. It seemed we were all uncertain where to begin.

'The thing that surprised me,' said James, 'was how much people liked your act.'

'Thank you very much,' Katherine shot back. 'It wasn't exactly meant for your taste.'

'Oh, I don't know,' he said, nudging her. 'What I meant was that you were much more confident than I expected. Both of you.'

'So everyone seemed to enjoy it?' asked Katherine, smiling.

'Not quite everyone,' said Albert.

I braced myself.

'What makes you say that?' said James. 'Everyone was having a fine time, as far as I could tell.'

'Mmm,' said Albert. 'You couldn't see, but there was a chap at the table next to me. Dark, stocky. He didn't clap; he just sat there screwing up his napkin.'

'Did you get a look at his face?' I asked. 'What was he wearing? What sort of man was he?'

'I couldn't see much of him. He was wearing a workman's blue jacket, and a flat cap pulled over his eyes. I only saw that he was dark-haired because it was past his collar at the back. Did you see anything?' he asked James.

James shook his head. 'No more than you. Now I think of it, I know the man you mean, but I didn't have a clear view. Anyway,' he nudged Katherine again, 'I was keeping the women at bay.' He eyed the bunch of peonies which Katherine was clutching. 'Perhaps I should be keeping your admirers at bay instead.'

'Whoever sent these is hardly that,' said Katherine. 'Peonies mean bad luck. I've brought them because they're evidence.'

'What did the note say?'

'That's the thing,' I said. 'There was a note, but it came later. And it was in the same writing as the first note, the one which came with the yellow roses. But now I don't think it did.'

James looked bewildered.

'I'm sorry,' I said. 'In fact, there were two notes.'

'Yes, you said that,' he replied, frowning.

'No, I mean tonight. A go-away note, sent to me this time — well, to "the singer" — and a note from Ellen Howe, asking us to stop looking for her.'

'Posted?' asked Albert.

'No. No postmark.'

'So at least she's safe, for now.' He paused. 'Do you intend to keep looking?'

'Yes!' Katherine cried. 'She's fled from her job, her livelihood. We need to find her.'

James took her hand. 'But what if you're leading this man to her?' he said, gently.

Katherine snatched her hand back. 'What am I supposed to do? Let her be frightened? Let her hide for ever?'

'Let me be devil's advocate,' said James. 'No crime's been committed. You two have been hanging round the music hall looking for evidence, and you've seen very little. The woman in question has asked you to stop.

118

You've both received threats. How much longer do you plan to keep this up?'

Katherine glared at him as if she would like to tie him in a knot.

'James is right, we can't do this much longer,' I said.

'Connie!' Her hurt expression pierced me to the heart, but I couldn't take the words back.

'It's true. I'm sorry, but it is. We have two notes, which we now know don't belong with the flowers. If you read them apart from the flowers, they're basically telling us to go away. For all we know, one of the other performers could have written them. I doubt they like having two posh newcomers as top of the bill. And soon, we won't be. I told Mother that I would return from Brighton this weekend. When I do, the act is finished.'

'But what about the man? What about Covent Garden?'

'What about it?' asked Albert, and I heard the exasperation in his voice.

'That's where the flowers must have come from,' argued Katherine. 'Covent Garden market, at the end of the day. How else could a working man afford to send flowers like that?'

James sighed, and studied his feet. 'All right,' he said, looking up. 'That's a lead I can follow up. But I might not be able to chaperone you two tomorrow if I do.' He glanced at Albert. 'Lamont, can you look after them for me?'

'We don't need looking after,' Katherine retorted.

'I can accompany you, if you prefer,' said Albert. 'I'd be intrigued to see your act again.' For the first time, I saw a hint of merriment in his face.

'If you do, please don't come in evening dress,'

snapped Katherine. 'You stuck out like a pair of sore thumbs.'

'Given what you were wearing, K, you're in no place to criticise my choice of outfit,' said Albert. 'Anyway, we're almost at yours now. Are you getting out too, King?'

James raised his eyebrows. 'I could.'

The carriage rolled to a stop, and Katherine got out, not waiting for James to help her. I could see her anger in the set of her shoulders. 'See you tomorrow,' she said, not looking round. 'Don't forget it's afternoon rehearsals.'

'I won't,' I said, although I wished I could. 'Goodnight.'

James shrugged. 'Good night, all.' He followed Katherine, slamming the carriage door behind him.

Tredwell shouted 'Hup!' to the horse, and we moved off. 'Home, sir?' he called.

Albert looked at me, and smiled. 'Yes please, Tredwell. Home it is.'

I had known that it would be. We had discussed the matter that morning. My trunk had been brought from Putney, and installed in the guest room. Yet it still felt unreal.

'What did your father say?' I asked.

Albert looked bashful. 'I think he was impressed at my cheek,' he admitted. 'Installing a woman down the corridor, he said.'

My hands flew to my mouth. 'He didn't!' I gasped.

Albert's arm crept round me. 'I'm afraid he did. But I promised him that I would behave and I shall, even though I don't want to. You're safer with me here than in some Putney hotel.'

'I'm not so sure,' I said. The carriage was warm and

snug, and the motion of the horses soothing. 'Was it —
was it very bad?' I whispered.

Albert's chin rested on the top of my head. 'Was what
very bad?'

'You know. The act. That song.'

'Noooooo.' A vigorous headshake. 'Funny, yes. A bit
rude, definitely yes.' I shifted round to look up at him. 'It
made me wonder —'

'Are you horrified?'

Albert tucked a loose strand of hair behind my ear. 'If
you'll let me finish, Constance Swift, it made me wonder
why I had never heard you sing before. I never knew you
could sing.'

'I can't, usually. I get nervous. I hate people looking at
me.'

Albert leaned close, and his breath tickled my ear. 'If I
promise not to look, would you sing for me? Not *that*
song,' he added hastily. 'Something different.'

I closed my eyes while my mind flicked through the
songs I knew, as if it were turning over sheet music at the
piano. Then I remembered the first time I had sung at the
music hall, standing in the wings with Katherine centre
stage.

'*The boy I love is up in the gallery*,' I sang. '*The boy I
love is looking now at me…*'

'No he isn't,' Albert whispered, and I heard the smile in
his voice.

'He can if he likes,' I whispered back.

***

We ate a late supper in the guest room; cold meat,
bread, and wine, drunk from the same glass. 'Are you sure
you don't mind coming tomorrow?' I asked.

121

Albert was sitting on the floor at my feet, leaning against the sofa. 'Of course not,' he said. 'It's a few days — how many days?'

I ticked them off on my fingers. 'Wednesday, Thursday, Friday, Saturday. Four. At most.'

'Mm. I'll have to speak to Tredwell tomorrow and see if I can borrow some clothes for the music hall. I certainly wouldn't want to stick out like a sore thumb, as K put it.'

I touched his shoulder. 'She didn't mean it. She's just —'

'Angry that we're not all going to support her stage act until the end of time.'

'That's rather harsh.'

'Perhaps. I think she's enjoying it more than you are, though.'

'It isn't for much longer,' I said. 'Four more days. Four more days to find the man, and solve the mystery.'

'And then…' Albert looked up at me, smiling.

'And then I shall go home, and endure endless nagging and dress fittings and arrangements, so that I can say "I will" to you.'

Albert winced. 'It sounds awful. How long does all that take?'

I cast my mind back to my sister's wedding. 'Jemima was engaged for two years.'

'Oh Lord.' Albert scrambled up to sit beside me. 'I can't wait for two years while your mother decides what dress she's wearing.'

***

Albert leaned forward. 'Tredwell, once the ladies have left the carriage, go round the corner. I need to get out separately.'

122

'You do,' said Katherine. 'You look disreputable, and —'

'That will do,' said Albert. 'Let your doorman know I'm not a prowler, if you don't mind.'

Tredwell had managed to procure corduroy trousers and a loose shirt for Albert, along with a dun-coloured jacket and a cap. Under the cap, his hair fell over his eyes, and he hadn't shaved that morning. 'You do look distinctly dangerous,' I murmured, 'but I rather like it.'

'Do shut up, Connie,' said Katherine, opening the carriage door.

We were slightly late, and the dressing-room was already full of people getting ready. There was an empty seat at the dressing table next to Selina, and she looked round as Katherine slid into it. 'Thought you might've had a better offer,' she said. 'All them flowers, an' that.'

'Oh, flowers,' said Katherine, wrinkling her nose as she unpinned her hat. 'I bet Ellen got heaps more flowers than me.'

'Nah,' said Selina. 'She was a funny one like that. Never mingled with the audience after the show, never went down an' got bought drinks an' supper or flowers. That's the whole point, ain't it, to be looked up to an' bought things?'

'I'd love to be bought things,' said Katherine. 'Maybe I should try it.'

Selina snorted. 'If you don't mind where they put their hands, that is. Maybe that was it. Seeing as her act was dressin' up as a little girl, it wouldn't have been quite nice for her to be sittin' on men's knees knocking back the gin.'

'I suppose not,' I said, feeling left out of the conversation. 'But flowers would be nice.'

Selina craned round to look at me. 'Ellen didn't think so. When she did get flowers, she usually gave 'em to us. Red roses like velvet, blushin' pink tulips, she didn't give a monkey's what they were.' She turned to the mirror. 'You'd better get moving, Felicity Velooer. That face won't paint itself.'

Katherine got up and went to the costume rail. She inspected the dresses, sliding the hangers down the rail. 'Come on,' I called. 'You've got a choice of two. Tartan or stripes.' She was looking at a short scarlet dress with white polka dots. 'That isn't a Felicity frock, it's too pretty.'

'I know,' she said, pushing it away. She returned with the tartan outfit, shrugged off her dress, and wriggled into it, frills, flounces and all. 'I'm starting to get used to it,' she said, examining her clashing reflection and reaching for a greasepaint stick.

Don't get too used to it, I thought. *Four days, and we're finished. Four days, and everything will be back to normal.*

But would the man who sent the flowers be finished?

And what about Ellen Howe, hiding in the shadows, scared we would find her?

I looked past the yellow roses, fading now, to the polka-dot dress on the rail.

What would become of Little Dottie Jones?

CHAPTER 16
Katherine

The curtain came down and swayed in the dust as the safety curtain trundled beyond it.

Muffled clapping and cheers followed us offstage as the cast broke formation and returned to the dressing room.

No flowers. No note. Nothing had gone awry tonight. The other girls had been good-natured. Even Mabel seemed to be thawing. Sally had come to ask in an undertone if she could be my understudy. She was a good mimic, could copy my accent and could also sing solo, if only Mr Templeton would let her. Sally had been one of the few who had always been welcoming.

'I want to better myself,' she said, still quietly. 'Being a dancer is easy work, I know that, and well-paid, but — well, it ain't for ever. And men think —' She bit her lip.

'What do men think?' I asked, speaking as quietly as she had done.

'I don't want men to think I'm a good-time girl,' she said. 'But cos you've been prancing about with 'alf your legs showing and then leave without an 'at, they think you're fair game. But I'm not like that.' She sighed. 'I miss Ellen. We used to leave together — safety in numbers and all that. I wish I was a lady like you…'

I gave Sally my hat to wear, telling her quite truthfully that I had another one at home and this one suited her better than it did me. Then I hooked my arm in hers, and with Connie we went to find Albert and Tredwell, who escorted us through the waiting strangers to the well-lit pavement. 'Will you be safe from here?' I asked.

A cab moved forward from the waiting line. 'I will now, Miss Caster,' said Sally, smiling. 'I've got enough to take a ride for once. Thank you for looking after me.' She hurried towards the cab.

'Well,' said Albert, once we settled inside the carriage. 'I've spent the whole evening wearing Tredwell's togs and found nothing but mostly jolly nice chaps out for beer and a laugh. Some are more gentlemanly than others, and by that I don't mean their social class. I recognised a couple of rotters from school, and if you like I can tell you which ones the girls need to watch out for. But no-one disliked your act — or if they did, they wouldn't say. I mentioned Little Dottie Jones and a few said they'd like to see her back, and others said they preferred women to girls. That's about it.'

Connie was cuddled up to Albert, gazing into his face. His hand was on her knee. I felt as if I was turning into Aunt Alice. Surely Albert wouldn't let his desires get the better of them. Although looking at them right now, Connie was the one who might need a bucket of cold water, and Albert whose honour might be in danger.

'I know it's not exactly the thing,' I said, 'but if we can pull up, I'm going to sit with Tredwell. It's too hot in here.'

126

The view from Tredwell's seat was magnificent. London, twinkling and smoky, spread out under thick opaque skies. We rattled over Lambeth Bridge and into Westminster, and then west towards Fulham. Other carriages, cabs and bicycles trundled along in a strange dance, following, dividing, rejoining. Lulled by the steady movement of the carriage and the rhythmic clopping of hooves, I felt myself growing sleepy.

'You ladies are a caution, and no mistake,' said Tredwell eventually. 'I mean no disrespect Miss Demeray, but while Miss Swift might need a hobby, I'm surprised you have the energy to gad about like this. What with having a job and helping out at home, and all.'

He had a point. I was exhausted. My day had started with light housework, I'd gone to Dr Farquhar's to do more typing, I'd snatched lunch with James while he told me his plans, I'd come home and helped with Margaret's homework, I'd perused Father's letter for the millionth time trying to work out if there was a secret message, I'd gone to the music hall. Aunt Alice had been out when I left. Ada, with narrowed lips, handed me the book on self-defence as I stepped through the front door. She must have found it in my room.

'I don't know why you should need this for dinner at Miss Swift's,' she'd said, 'but as, yet again, you're not in an evening dress, I assume it may be useful.' Her fierce expression softened for a total of two seconds. 'Be careful, Miss Kitty,' she'd whispered, and then her brows beetled again. 'And don't be as late back as you were last night.'

Now, swaying above the horses, I said, 'Did you find anything out, Tredwell?'

'Not much, truth to tell,' he said, 'Ellen's got a good

reputation. She may be a little saucy on stage, but that's it. Nothing more to find out. Here you are, safe home. Your folks keep late hours, look at all them lights on.'

He was right. I descended with a sense of deep dread and stood on the pavement as the carriage rattled off to take Connie to safety. I had a sudden urge to rush after them and beg to go with them.

My key nearly broke in the lock as the door was wrenched open.

Aunt Alice stood quivering. I'd never seen her angry before and she had lived with us for fourteen years.

'Katherine Mathilda Demeray, you will be the death of me!' she snapped, the closest she'd ever come to raising her voice. 'What sort of example are you setting your sister? What would your father say? I have a good mind to lock you in your room!'

I was too tired and dispirited to respond with any grace. 'I was twenty-six in May,' I snapped. 'I can do what I like and I am too old to be locked up anywhere.'

'Have you no respect for your mother's memory?'

'Don't bring Mother into this.'

'This is the fourth night you have been out till all hours, coming back smelling peculiar and with paint in your ears. Yesterday there were grass-stains on your best petticoat. Do you think I'm blind or stupid? What are you really doing? I refuse to believe you've been going to dinner parties at the Swifts. Firstly, you're in one of your housework dresses and you have no hat. Secondly, I read in the paper that the Swifts were attending a ball last night *without Miss Constance Swift who is staying from home.*'

Oh dear. Why hadn't Connie mentioned that?

I put my things down on the hall stand, trying to think

up an excuse. There was an envelope in James's handwriting on the salver. I was tempted to tell the truth, since keeping up or rather, failing to keep up with all this pretence was exhausting. But I couldn't. Aunt Alice would probably dispatch me to some relation in the country who would teach me demureness, obedience and invisibility. The thought of her forcing me onto a train combined with my utter weariness and I started to giggle.

'There is nothing whatsoever to laugh about. I am ashamed of you.'

I took a breath and said 'Aunt Alice, I can't explain properly, not now. But it's to do with…' I caught sight of my hatless head in the mirror. 'We're helping James rescue girls who are at risk of being forced into immoral employment.'

We stood in silence. I knew without looking that Margaret was staring through the banisters and that Ada was listening from the attic.

Aunt Alice deflated a little. There were tears in her eyes, and I wondered if this was affecting her in ways of which I was unaware.

'We shall discuss this in the morning, Katherine. I suggest you go to bed now. Ada put out hot water for you a short while ago. Hopefully it is still warm.'

I slipped James's letter into my bag and went to my room. My bed looked so inviting. I stripped down to my chemise and drawers and washed thoroughly, until all traces of make-up and cream were removed, then I let down my hair and started to brush it while I read James's note. It had been sent by the evening post.

6pm. Dear Katherine, I have information from Somerset House. Am going to CG now with a name. I

*should be finished before you get back from your evening
out and are fast asleep, and I'll put a note under your door
to let you know all's well. Lunch tomorrow? Yours J.*

I listened. The house was silent. It was impossible to
look down on the pavement from my window but surely if
James had been near I'd have seen him. I slipped
downstairs barefoot and looked out of the window.
Nothing. I prodded around the bottom of the door. No note.

I went upstairs and sat in front of the mirror. My
candle-lit reflection had circles under her eyes and looked
fit to drop. But I felt restless. Where was James?

There was nothing for it. I pinned my hair in a flat
plaited circle. Creeping out to the airing cupboard, I found
Margaret's cycling knickerbockers and an old shirt of
Father's which I sometimes wore for the dustier sort of
spring cleaning. His soft hat was in the hall cupboard.

I have never cycled so fast before or since. The roads
were quiet at first, but as I went further into London, I had
to weave to avoid cabs, carriages, and knots of laughing
people spilling out of pubs and theatres.

A cab cut in behind me and the driver shouted 'Hoy!
Mind where you're going!'

I considered what level of rudeness to use in my reply,
and looked over my shoulder to deliver it. But I never did,
because in the glare of the cab-lamps I recognised Sam
Webster, and his eyes widened as he recognised me.

'Pull up!' he shouted, and we suffered the wrath of
every other vehicle on the road.

'You again,' he said. 'Where to, now? I take it it's not a
social call, given your togs.'

'Covent Garden.'

'You gotta be kidding. At this time? What you looking

for there?'

'My . . . Mr King. I think he may be in danger.'

'Lor luvva duck. Can't you all take up choir practice? I'm not heading to Covent Garden this time of night on my own, nor am I letting *you* wander round alone. And I can't leave the cab. I'd come back and find nothing but hoof-prints.'

'I'm dressed as a boy. I'll be fine.'

'You really are an innercent, ain't yer, Miss? Hop in, and I'll knock up one of my chums at the shelter in Leicester Square to tag along. One with a cosh.'

***

Covent Garden was in total darkness. I hadn't ever been there, but it was hard to associate it with bright flowers and fresh vegetables up from the country. The buildings loomed and the stench of rotten vegetation filled the hot summer air. Shadows shifted in narrow alleys.

'You sure he's here?' said Sam.

I was. I couldn't explain how I knew, but James was somewhere nearby. My heart thudded as I stepped down onto the cobbles.

'Come on then,' said Sam, taking down one of the lanterns. 'Keep your eyes peeled, Arnie, or they'll steal the 'ooves off the 'orse.'

We walked slowly, Sam shining the lantern into nooks and crannies. In a doorway was what looked like a bundle of dumped rags, but I had seen those clothes, those worn shoes before.

I ran to the doorway. 'Wait!' cried Sam. 'Let me come alonger you, it ain't safe.' But I had already knelt by the curled figure and pulled back enough of its covering to see that it was James.

'Is 'e…?'

'He's breathing,' I said. 'Help me, Sam.'

'We oughta get a doctor.'

'We need to get him home first.'

James gave a hoarse murmur at the sound of my voice and lifted his hand towards me. There was no blood around his head or on his clothes. His face in the lantern light looked strange and it took me a moment to realise he had shaved off his moustache. I traced the stubble where it had been.

'Come on, sir,' said Sam and hefted James up out of the doorway. James half walked, half dragged himself into the cab, where he slumped in silence.

'Back to yours?' said Sam, 'or back to his?'

'No, to Mr Lamont's,' I said. 'Albert has more space to manage this sort of thing.' I couldn't face explaining anything else to Aunt Alice.

The cab moved and James, lolling against me, whispered something I couldn't catch. He touched his throat and tried again.

'Remind me to buy a better hat.'

'Oh James,' I whispered, even though there was no-one to hear us, 'oh my darling.' I held him tight, feeling his heart slowly thudding through my thin clothes, his hands so cold despite the hot night.

When we arrived at Albert's it took a while for the servants to find him, and when they did, he seemed more put out than I'd expected. All the same, he said he'd make sure James was looked after and sent me home, paying Sam triple his fare.

At home, however, it didn't look as if sneaking in would be easy. Policemen and men in overcoats were walking about with lanterns.

'What's going on?' said Sam to one of them as we turned the corner. The man pointed to a figure crumpled on the ground. A small woman in a neat dark dress stared sightlessly into the night, her tongue poking out. Half-fallen from her head and caught in her reddish-brown hair was a hat. It was the one I'd given away four hours earlier.

CHAPTER 17
Connie

The bed was comfortable, and the guest room was warm, but still I lay awake.

Tonight's performance had gone well. I had expected — something. Another note, and another bouquet of flowers for Katherine. But nothing untoward had happened.

The dressing room had been more harmonious than usual, as far as I could judge. Katherine had chatted and joked with the other performers, and as usual, I had been a fish out of water. A couple of people had said hello, or asked me to move so that they could pass, and that had been about it. Katherine had been busy talking to Selina, and later to Sally, who seemed to look up to her. Just as on stage, I was on the sidelines; the only person who stood still, while everyone else danced by.

It had been a relief when Katherine had gone to sit with Tredwell on the journey home. Once or twice, while Albert told us what he had learnt, I caught her looking at me in an unnerving manner, as if she wanted to turn me inside out. We had barely spoken all evening. I wished that this whole experience was over, and we could be just friends again. Even when she was outside with Tredwell I felt tense and jumpy, as if she might pop her head through the window at any minute and glare at me. I shivered, and huddled closer to Albert.

'Are you all right, Connie?' he asked, putting his arm around me. 'You're very quiet.'

'I'm a little tired,' I murmured. It was more than that. Everything was pulling me different ways, and my emotions were a mixture of desire and sadness and loneliness and fear and, sometimes, elation. But how could I tell Albert that?

Our routine at the house was the same as the previous night; a late supper and a glass of wine in my room, while discussing the evening. By mutual consent, we sat at opposite ends of the sofa. Eventually the wine was gone. Albert set the glass on the tray, and glanced at me. 'I'd better go,' he said, reaching for my hand. 'We both need sleep.'

'I wish you didn't have to leave.' The words were out of my mouth before I realised what I'd said, and I gasped. 'I mean — I mean you couldn't, but it isn't that I don't want to —' I gabbled, my face on fire and looking everywhere but at him.

'Connie…' He crouched beside me, and cupped my face in his hands. 'I would love to stay, but as you say, I can't.' He kissed me, and I did my best not to cling to him, to smile and let him go.

And yet here I was, still awake.

**

The knock at the door rang out like a gunshot. I froze, then pulled the covers over my head, like a little girl

135

playing hide-and-seek. *If I can't see you, you can't see me.* I strained my ears. Footsteps, a creak, then voices, low at first, then rising.

Someone came upstairs. What — who did they want? They grew louder, and with every creak my heart beat as if it would jump out of my chest.

A knock, and I almost screamed. What if it was the police, or my father? I would be dragged out and shamed. But then I heard a soft voice. 'Master Albert, sir, you're wanted. Master Albert, sir…'

A door opening. 'What is it?' asked Albert, and I could tell from his voice that he had not slept either.

'It's — well, your cousin Miss Demeray has arrived, and she has a man with her, in a bad way. He needs medical attention.'

'K's here? Wait a minute.' A pause, then steps running down the corridor, running away.

When I was sure the coast was clear, I opened my door a fraction and peeped out. I couldn't see much, but the voices were clearer. Katherine's words tumbling one after the other, Albert's slower speech. The man with Katherine could only be James, surely, but I couldn't hear him at all. Albert's voice, slightly raised now. 'No, K, you can't stay.' Then, more gently, 'Your aunt would be worried sick. You must go home, and Sam will take you.' Katherine's voice again, but feebler, and the gentle click of the door.

There was silence for a moment, and then someone came from another part of the house. A deep, loud voice spoke. 'What's this, Bertie? Another waif and stray?'

'Father, this is James King who was at Eton with me. He's been attacked, and needs a doctor.'

'Yes, but why is he here? And why is he dressed like a

tramp?' An exasperated snort. 'On second thoughts, I don't want to know. You can deal with him, but hear me. This has to stop. This, and the — other business.' I could imagine the look of contempt in the direction of my room. 'It all has to stop.' And the footsteps stamped back the way they had come.

After a pause I heard Albert's voice, gentle. 'Come on, James. Dinsdale, can you give me a hand to get him upstairs? That's it.' A series of creaks and huffs marked their progress up the stairs. 'Nearly there.'

'Where shall we put him, Master Albert? In the blue room?' My heart skipped a beat. The room I was in had blue walls and cornflower-patterned hangings.

'No, not that one,' Albert said quickly. 'Put him in the Chinese room so that he's next to me.' And I breathed again.

A door opened, very near, and bedsprings creaked. 'It's all right, James,' Albert said. 'You're in my house, and we'll fetch a doctor. Everything will be all right.'

'Where's Katherine?' I scarcely recognised James's voice. 'She was with me, but —'

'She's fine, James, I've sent her home in a cab. She's safe. Try and rest.'

I peeped out. The corridor was deserted. Then Albert appeared in a dressing-gown. 'Albert,' I whispered. He looked round, and for a moment he didn't seem to recognise me. 'What's happened to James?'

'Some ruffian tried to strangle him. K found him in a doorway in Covent Garden.' His voice was curt. 'I'll get someone to fetch Farquhar.'

A wave of guilt broke over me. I had barely thought of James all evening. He had run a risk in going alone to

Covent Garden, to help us. He could have been killed. 'Shall I sit with him till the doctor comes?'

Albert's expression softened. 'Yes please, Connie. I'll be back as soon as I can.' A sudden smile lit up his exhausted face as he looked at me. 'You might want to fetch your dressing-gown first, though. You'll catch a cold.' I gasped, wrapped my arms around myself, and glared at him, but it had no effect at all.

***

James's eyes followed me as I poured a glass of water. 'Very strange dream,' he whispered.

'I'm afraid it's real,' I said. 'Do you need help to sit up?'

He nodded. 'What are you doing here?' he asked, as I supported him to a sitting position.

'Where's your moustache?' I countered.

He touched his upper lip, frowning. 'Oh yes. I thought the man from the music hall might know me, with it.' Even those few words were an effort, and he swallowed the water gratefully.

'Did you see who attacked you?'

James shook his head. 'Behind me. I was in the market, and then —' He mimed hands around his neck. He didn't have to. Purple bruises ringed his neck, a garland of hate.

'Did you see the man from the music hall?'

He shook his head, and closed his eyes. His hair fell over his brow, and I smoothed it back. Without the moustache, James looked years younger; his man-about-town air was quite gone. Propped up on the pillows he seemed fragile, paper-thin. 'Try to sleep,' I whispered.

His eyes opened. 'Katherine was dressed as a boy, you know,' he said, almost conversationally. 'Is it a new act?'

I started as Albert came in. 'Tredwell's gone to get Farquhar,' he murmured. 'How's he doing?'

'Was Katherine dressed as a boy?' I asked.

Albert looked sidelong at me. 'Yes, she was. And no, I don't know why.'

We sat side by side, keeping a silent vigil as James slept and the candle burned down. I hid in my room when Dr Farquhar came, and listened at the door as the doctor pronounced James's injuries relatively minor. 'Not that I'd want them myself, you understand,' he said. 'How did he come to be like this?'

'Undercover work,' said Albert, firmly.

'Well, he needs to rest for a day or two, and give the injury time to heal. No undercover missions, no heroic crusades. All that can wait.' The sound of a doctor's bag being secured. 'Shall I send my bill to you?'

'Please,' said Albert. 'I'll see you out.'

I retreated to my room, and fell into a fitful sleep, full of footsteps and voices and comings and goings and people dressed in the wrong clothes. Once or twice I started awake, and wondered where I was, and it took me a few minutes to work it out. Albert's father's words echoed in my head: 'This has to stop.' *He's right,* I thought, and it brought a strange sort of comfort. Perhaps then things would return to normal.

The next moment I was jolted awake. 'Connie, get dressed. Quickly.'

Albert was shaking my shoulder, his fingers warm through the thin cotton of my nightgown. I gasped. 'You shouldn't be —'

'Never mind that.' He thrust a newspaper under my nose. 'A woman was murdered in Katherine's street last night. A small, red-haired woman.'

I stared at him, aghast, then leapt out of bed and snatched last night's dress.

This has to stop.

CHAPTER 18
Katherine

'Oh, Katherine.'

I woke with a start. Light fringed the edges of the curtains and from outside came sounds of traffic.

I sat up and found Connie standing at my side with a tray. What on earth…? I rubbed my eyes, but she was still there. 'What time is it?'

'Just after ten.' She put the tray down on my dressing table and came to sit on the edge of the bed. 'How are you?'

Just after ten? I was still in the middle of a dream. Confused images raced around in my head; dark shadows, looming buildings, huddled bodies.

'Your aunt thinks you need rest. Have some tea. Do you want me to open the curtains?'

'Yes, please.'

I lifted the cup and my trembling hand spilt tea into the saucer. It hadn't been a dream. I had found James left for dead in a doorway. Sally's body really had lain on the corner of our street with my old hat caught in her hair. I had slipped in through our back door while the police were knocking on our neighbour's front door, knowing I would be lucky to get to my room before anyone woke. But I managed it. Margaret's knickerbockers and Father's shirt were thrown into the wardrobe, then I dived into bed and waited for the police to arrive at our house.

When the knock came I could barely distinguish it from my own pulse thudding. And my heart nearly broke when I heard Aunt Alice's panicked voice in the hallway. 'A young woman? A short red-headed woman?' She had never raised her voice before, but her wail of '*Katherine! Margaret!*' was as anguished as a mother's.

I was glad that I could call downstairs to let her know I was safe, that bleary-eyed Margaret was on the lower landing as I descended, and that moments later all of us were together, huddled in the hall. Then I had to confirm that the hat Sally had worn was mine, and that I had given it to her, and I realised she was never going to be safe in anyone's loving arms again.

'Don't cry,' said Connie. 'I never know what to do when you cry. It's like trying to comfort an angry cat.'

'Sally was murdered last night.'

'I know. It's why Albert brought me here.'

'Albert? Why did he bring you, rather than Hodgkins? Connie, what aren't you telling me?'

Connie squirmed and looked at her hands. She was as immaculately dressed as always but her hair, as it had for a few days, had the same haphazard style which suggested she'd done it herself.

'Connie, please tell me you're not in some awful boarding house. You could have stayed here. I've have explained to Aunt Alice somehow. How could you? I don't want your death on my conscience, too.'

'Sally's death is not your fault. And if I want to stay in a boarding house, I can.' She rose and went to stare out of the window.

'I gave her my hat,' I said. 'Whoever did this thought she was me. When that cab pulled up next to Sally . . . I think the killer was inside.'

Connie turned, her mouth open. 'You must stop this now! We're risking so much, and it's getting worse and worse.' She caught sight of my raised eyebrows, and her face darkened. 'It isn't just you, you know!'

We stared at each other. How had we come to this point? Then Connie's gaze wavered. 'I've had enough,' she muttered.

'Connie, I'm sorry,' I said. 'I didn't mean to imply you were any less involved. But — you're not telling me anything, and I feel so lost without your help.'

Connie still wouldn't look at me. 'You manage so well, and you're so confident. I don't think you need me at all.'

'That's not true. I'm not confident! Why does everyone think I'm confident? I just cope. It's what I do. It's what I've done since Mother died, since Father disappeared. I cope. Someone has to pretend everything's all right. I didn't want it to be me, but it is. Then you turned up and I had someone to share it with, but now...'

'Well I thought so too, only last night you wouldn't even sit with me. You went to sit with Tredwell.'

'But that wasn't...' I threw back the covers and went to her. 'You and Albert looked as if you wanted to be alone. Very much alone. I didn't know where to look.'

Connie's face went red, but there was a tiny smile.

I said, 'I wish you'd just get married.' She blinked.

'You seem so in love and it's as if you need to…' I petered out.

Her eyes were twinkling. 'Perhaps we do. The truth is, I've been staying at the Lamonts' house.' She burst out laughing. 'Oh Katherine, your face!'

She hooked her arm into mine and we sat on the edge of the bed.

'I know you can keep a secret. I found a respectable hotel, but Albert caught me seeing you home from the music hall. His horses were tired, so I couldn't get to the hotel, and of course I couldn't go home, as I was meant to be in Brighton. So he took me to his home instead, as a matter of safety. And no, we haven't done anything your inner maiden aunt would disapprove of, unless you count eating supper together. But . . . he proposed!' She looked up at me, and her happiness was mingled with guilt. 'I'm sorry I didn't tell you; it just never seemed to be the right moment. Only I'm not quite sure what happens now.' Her face dropped a little. 'I don't want all that wedding fuss. I just want to…'

'Please don't tell me what you "just want to do",' I said. 'I'm not that naive.'

I was pleased for them, so pleased. From almost the moment I'd introduced Connie to my cousin, I'd known they were perfect for each other. In the midst of the fear and violence and humiliation of the last few days, something lovely had come out of it all. I was so happy for her, but a tiny voice said 'always the bridesmaid' and I saw a future in which I helped to look after Margaret's children, because no-one thought I was lovable enough to be a wife. I was the woman whom a man would snatch kisses from in a cab, because he could.

'It'll be you and James next,' she said, as if reading my thoughts. 'I helped nurse him last night. I know it should have been you nursing him, but I was all they had. He's doing well but he's still a little confused. Not so confused he couldn't write to you though. He loves you very much.'

'Did he say so?'

'Of course not. He wasn't bashed on the head so hard he'd talk about his feelings. But he was bashed enough to be serious.' She rummaged in her bag and then paused. 'You mustn't tell about the proposal.'

'No, of course not.'

I took the note and opened it. There was one sheet of paper with James's familiar script, more sprawling than normal, and another folded piece within.

I stopped myself in time from reading the first aloud. It said *Glad you've taken to picking up tramps. Looking forward to your next song which should be entitled 'Oh no I forgot me corset'. Your darling James.*

'What does it say?' said Connie.

'I think he's thanking me for finding him.' How had he known I wasn't wearing a corset? The man must have magical powers. I restrained a smirk.

I opened the other piece of paper. It was in his usual handwriting, neat and succinct. 'This must be what he found out in Somerset House,' I said. His notes were set out in rows.

Birth March 3 1866 Lindenhowe Somerset to John Edward Henderson (farm labourer) and May Dorothy Henderson nee Jones (housewife), a daughter Helen May.

Entry in newspaper 1881 re: an incident in Seven Dials. One of the witnesses named as Helen Henderson living as a lodger in a nearby property. Profession: seamstress in Covent Garden Theatre.

Marriage Sept 15 1885 Marylebone Register Office: Caleb Brown, costermonger address in Seven Dials and Helen May Henderson different address in Seven Dials, seamstress.

Birth Jan 3 1887 to Caleb (costermonger) and Helen Brown nee Henderson (seamstress) living in Soho, a daughter Mary Amelia.

'That's who James was looking for,' I said. 'Ellen Howe is as much of a false name as Dottie Jones. James was looking for Caleb Brown, husband of Helen Brown, because Helen Brown is Ellen Howe and either he knows where she is or...'

I thought for a moment, trying to piece it together.

'Selina said that Ellen keeps her distance from men. Does it mean she's afraid of them? She is married, and she has a child. On the other hand, she took the baby back to the country and left her with family there. Does that mean she was afraid of her husband? If so, why didn't she stay in Somerset? Did she miss him? Before the baby came, she worked in the theatre, though not as a performer. We've got to return to Covent Garden, but in daylight. It can't be as bad in the daylight.'

Connie was twisting her hands. She'd had enough. I was stopping her from organising her wedding to the sort of man she'd never have to run from. I didn't want to cope on my own, but it wasn't fair to make her feel obliged to investigate with me.

'Connie, if you don't want to keep searching for Ellen, I understand.'

146

'Is that what you want?'

'No! I want your help. I *need* your help. But I don't want you to give it because you think you have to.'

'I don't think that at all. I thought you were letting me tag along to be nice.'

How had we got to this point? I shook my head and looked round the room and something made me pause. I remembered shoving Father's soft hat under the washstand, but it wasn't there. Perhaps I'd put it in the wardrobe. I got up and looked inside but it wasn't there either. Nor were the knickerbockers and shirt. Ada had been in. Or Aunt Alice. One of them knew I'd been out last night after I'd supposedly gone to bed.

'We've got into a right to-do with each other,' said Connie. 'I think it's the heat. It's not even eleven o'clock and I can't think straight. Can we start again?'

I looked in the mirror at her reflection, sitting anxious as she used to and still the dearest friend I'd ever had. She was right about the weather. My head was thumping.

'Of course we can,' I said. 'I'm sorry if I've seemed distant. It's just that I felt you'd rather be with Albert.'

Connie grinned, her eyes twinkling, then pulled a face. 'It's not that really, but I just don't take to music hall life like you do,' she said. 'Can you imagine me on Mr Templeton's knee?'

'Perhaps we should suggest it as a change.' We burst out laughing.

'By the way,' said Connie, wiping her eyes, 'I told your aunt that we were working undercover to rescue fallen women. I hope that's not far off whatever you told her. She seemed to swallow it, and it's almost true. And . . . can I stay here till we've finished at the music hall? It would be

147

safer, for both of us. I can't stay at Albert's any longer in case…'

'You become a fallen woman yourself?'

She blushed, that same soft smile on her face.

'Don't tell me you've never thought of it all those times you've been on your own with James,' she said.

'Never,' I said. 'Well, Connie, we've got work to do and I need a bath first. And maybe you do too. Preferably,' I added, 'a cold one.'

CHAPTER 19
Connie

I looked at Katherine and Albert, standing at James's bedside. 'We have to go to the police,' I said, and everyone looked at me.

'Connie's right,' James said huskily, and began to get out of bed.

'No you don't,' said Katherine, laying a hand on his chest. 'You're convalescing. And now that I know how to wrestle you into submission, don't think I won't.'

I glanced across at Albert, sitting on the opposite side of the bed, but he wasn't smiling. His hands were clasped together in his lap, and the knuckles showed white. 'Yes,' he said, slowly. 'I suppose we have to involve the police. We can go and talk to Barnes. He'll be discreet.' I remembered his father's words last night — or was it early this morning? — about waifs and strays and the 'other business'. If any of our activities got into the papers, I suspected Albert would suffer.

'How were your meetings?' I asked, to divert him. When we had arrived at the Lamont house, the butler had informed us that Albert was 'from home, on business', and it had taken all Katherine's powers of persuasion to get us into the house. Even so, we had had to wait in the morning room, kicking our heels, until Albert returned half an hour later and rescued us. He had seemed abstracted, shaking my hand in greeting, and I had put it down to his mind still being on business matters.

'Meetings?' He stared at me as if he had never heard the word before. 'Oh. Quite all right. Thank you.' I wondered if the investments in gold and copper and steel had worked out as he had hoped. Perhaps not, judging from his expression.

'Very well,' I said. 'We'll go and see Chief Inspector Barnes. We have a name now, thanks to James. We have a motive that makes sense. Let's get this mess dealt with.' I was surprised by the decisiveness of my own speech. But no-one else was willing to take the lead. Katherine and James were too busy gazing at each other, and Albert seemed to have his mind on his business empire rather than the business at hand. 'But first I'll go and pack.'

Albert came out of his reverie. 'Pack?' he snapped. 'What for? Where are you going?'

'To stay with Katherine until Sunday, as you won't let me go back to the hotel.'

'Aha, shenanigans,' said James. He attempted a smirk, winced, then shrank into his pillow as Albert and I both glared at him.

'It's clearly the sensible thing to do,' said Albert. 'I'll leave you to it. I have business to attend to, and I suppose you'll want escorting tonight, since King's out of action.'

'More business?' I asked, turning, but he had already gone.

Katherine helped me fold my clothes and fit them into the trunk. 'This isn't yours, is it?' She took a brush from the trunk and handed it to me.

I ran my fingers over the letters *AL* inlaid in the back. 'It's Albert's.' I laid it on the dressing table.

'Pinching his hairbrush,' Katherine remarked, rolling a pair of stockings. 'Things have moved on.'

'Indeed,' I said. I wasn't going to rise to Katherine's humour.

She moved closer. 'Have you agreed a date?' she asked, in an undertone.

'No.' I busied myself with folding petticoats and underthings, smoothing out the creases, making sure all was straight and neat. I wished I could smooth out the turmoil in my own mind. There was no wedding date. No engagement ring. No plans. The only place the wedding existed was in my head and in Albert's. And now in Katherine's. I wished I had never told her. I felt as if the bond between Albert and I had somehow grown thinner since last night, and his behaviour today did not reassure me. Already our gentle, intimate evenings together seemed like a dream. I shook my head to try and clear that thought away. 'Come on,' I said, bundling everything into the trunk and closing the lid. 'We should go.'

'I'll find Albert, and tell him we're leaving,' said Katherine, hurrying out.

I sat on the bed and stared at the trunk, biting my lip to keep back tears. I did not want to go to Katherine's house. I had already sat through a stiff lunch with Aunt Alice that day. She had made several references to the ball I had missed, and said she was sorry I hadn't been able to attend. It was more of a question than a statement. 'I wouldn't want to think that you were doing something inadvisable,' she had said, crumbling her bread roll absently. 'You girls have no idea how much worry you can put your elders through.' I told myself that she had had a terrible scare that morning, and that she was quite within her rights to be cross; but it still stung. 'And I am sure you will help Katherine,' she had said, as she left the table. 'Ada cannot do it all.'

Katherine and I exchanged glances. 'She'll come round,' said Katherine. But I wasn't so sure.

Tredwell and a footman came upstairs for the trunk. I lingered a moment in the room, running my hand over the bedspread, and the arm of the sofa where Albert and I had talked. 'Come along, Connie.' Katherine slipped her arm through mine. 'It's time to go.'

Albert was waiting downstairs for us. 'Can you manage without me?' he said. 'I have things to be getting on with. Tredwell can look after you. If Barnes wants to see me, he's welcome to call.'

'What about tonight?' I asked quietly. 'Will you be able to accompany us?'

'Is there any point in you going?' he asked. 'You're handing this over to the police, aren't you?'

'Of course there's a point!' said Katherine. 'We made a commitment and we intend to honour it.'

Albert looked at me, and while I longed to look away, I did not. His gaze flickered, breaking the moment. 'Then yes, I shall accompany you tonight.' He pressed my hand briefly and walked off.

'He's in a funny mood,' said Katherine. 'Let's go and sort this out.'

'Yes,' I said. I let Katherine lead me to the waiting

carriage, and got in. I looked out of the window, and a curtain twitched on the second floor. Someone was watching us leave. Albert's father flashed into my mind. And as the carriage began to move, I wondered if I would ever return.

***

Chief Inspector Barnes puffed out a breath as his eyes skimmed his notes. 'If this all adds up,' he said, 'it'll be one of the quickest collars in the history of the division.'

It hadn't felt quick. We had spent over an hour in a side room at Scotland Yard, while the Chief Inspector and a colleague had probed and questioned and challenged, and the notes James had made had been double-checked. When his colleague left the room, the Chief Inspector leaned forward. 'Why didn't you come to me sooner?' He sounded almost accusing.

'We — well, it wasn't a crime,' I said, and swallowed. 'We didn't particularly want anyone to know what we'd been doing.'

The Chief Inspector glanced at his notes again, and his mouth twitched. 'I can see why,' he remarked. 'If secretarying for Dr Farquhar ever grows dull, Miss Demeray, at least you have another string to your bow.' He closed his notebook. 'We'll go and find this Caleb Brown, and see what he has to say for himself. He shouldn't be too hard to track down.' He paused. 'Where should I direct any communication?'

'To me, please,' said Katherine, giving her address. 'Or in the evening, to Miss Caster at the Merrymakers Music Hall.'

His mouth twitched again. 'I'll see what I can do. Good day to you both.' We shook hands, and a uniformed officer

153

escorted us to the carriage.

Katherine got in first, and slumped in her seat. 'What a relief,' she breathed. 'Now we just need to find Ellen, tell her the good news, and retire from the stage.' She looked across. 'I'd have thought you would be jumping for joy, Connie, but you look as if you've lost a shilling and found sixpence. If that.'

'I'm just tired,' I said, and looked out of the window.

***

I stared at James, standing in Katherine's hall. 'Where's Albert?' I demanded, before realising how rude that made me seem. 'I mean, aren't you supposed to be resting?'

'I sound worse than I feel,' croaked James. 'Anyway, Dinsdale's with me in the carriage. He seems like a useful man in a crisis.'

He hadn't answered my question, and I couldn't ask again. Not in company. Presumably whatever business Albert had was more important than making sure we were safe. Or perhaps he didn't care. 'I would have thought —' I burst out, then stopped. Even if he had changed his mind about me, I would have thought he would protect his cousin. Perhaps I had been wrong.

'Connie, let me escort you to the carriage.' James took my arm and steered me outside. 'Don't be too hard on Albert,' he muttered. 'He wouldn't tell me why he couldn't come, but he's usually a man of his word.'

'That's what makes it worse,' I said, and practically towed James to the carriage.

I spent most of the journey to the music hall plotting an elaborate revenge which involved dressing in the shortest skirt I could find, painting my face, and singing one of Katherine's songs, adapted for the situation, all the while pointing at Albert.

I'm a lady you know,
I take afternoon tea
And I'll never put up
With a hand on my knee,
But Al persevered,
He can't be a gent,
Put his arm round my waist
And my hat got all bent...

But no-one would have laughed, I wouldn't have dared do it, and Albert wouldn't be there.

The dressing-room was subdued tonight. The news had got round about Sally. 'I saw her get in the cab,' wailed Betty. 'An' I thought "You lucky thing, getting a lift home."'

'You weren't to know,' said Katherine, putting a soothing hand on her arm. Betty gave her a surprised look, and burst into tears.

'At least you saw her safe to the cab,' said Mabel. 'You do care, dontcher? I can see you bin crying too. I . . . never mind.' She picked up the rouge and walked off.

I frowned over the sheet of paper I had borrowed. If I couldn't denounce Albert publicly myself, at least I could put words into Katherine's mouth. 'Here,' I said, scribbling the last line and pushing the sheet towards her. 'You can learn this for the second set.'

Katherine's eyes skimmed the page, and she giggled. 'That's rather cheeky, Connie.'

'If he doesn't keep his promises…'

Our first set of songs went well. I had persuaded

Katherine to swap 'The Boy I Love' for a different song. 'I can't face singing it again,' I said. 'I'm sick of it.' In truth, my voice would have cracked on the first note, and my heart would have broken with it.

We came offstage, and Katherine raced to the dressing-room to change for her dummy act. A moment after she had left to go back on, a knock at the door. 'Telegram for Miss — well, Miss Caster, but she said give it to the singer.'

I went to the door, and took it from Ron. 'Thank you,' I said, and ripped it open.

Brown has cast-iron alibi STOP Not our man STOP Released without charge STOP Maybe next time STOP Barnes

I stared into space. If Caleb Brown hadn't killed Sally… Who else would have done it? Why would anyone want to strangle an innocent young girl?

'That went well,' panted Katherine, pulling her cap and wig off in one movement.

Wordlessly, I passed her the telegram. She read it, and her jaw dropped. For a moment she looked like the wooden puppet she had been playing. Then she recovered herself. 'We need to think,' she said. 'This isn't over. Help me get my dress on, Connie.'

I moved mechanically, buttoning Katherine's dress, and re-pinning her hair into the loose style she wore as Felicity Velour. 'I'm glad James is out there,' she said, rubbing her arms as if she was cold. 'Do you still want to sing — that song you wrote?'

I nodded. 'Maybe it will cheer us up.'

As it turned out, we never did sing that song. The band were playing the opening bars when a shout came from the main doors. 'Stop the show!'

Ron dashed in, with Mr Templeton on his heels. 'Ladies and gentlemen —'

Mr Templeton pushed him aside. 'There has been an incident,' he said. 'The police are on their way. Everyone stay calm. You are safe, and once names have been taken, you can leave.' He looked at the stage. 'Sing something nice, you two,' he said, and disappeared.

We worked through our repertoire of ballads and folk songs until I was nearly hoarse. But finally three policemen arrived, and the crowd began to disperse. 'Thank you, ladies,' called Mr Templeton. 'Well done.'

Katherine walked to meet him. 'What happened?'

He sighed, and underneath the paint he looked very serious. 'Betty took Buster to do his business in the alley, and she saw what she thought was an old sack. She went closer and thought it might be a tramp, so she went to give 'im a kick and tell him to move on.'

He swallowed. 'It weren't a tramp,' he said, his voice almost as hoarse as James's. 'It fell forward at her feet. It's Ellen, and she's stone dead.'

CHAPTER 20
Katherine

James had come round to tell me the latest news. My heart lurched when I saw him, still grey, bruises showing above his collar, tired but at least fully conscious and on his feet. Despite all that had happened and my own sleepless night, the sight of him made me smile. I would have flung myself into his arms if next door's maid hadn't been peeking. James raised his hat, I nodded in greeting and let him in. Behind the door, he gave me a quick embrace and kissed my cheek.

'I wish…' He stepped away as we heard Aunt Alice coming up from the kitchen. 'The police came round to Albert's with more news of the murder,' he whispered. 'Can we talk in private?'

I sobered and ushered him into the drawing room.

'Poor Ellen,' I said. I felt nothing but guilt. If I hadn't been meddling, she'd still be alive.

'It wasn't Ellen,' said James. 'In the dark it looked like Ellen, and everyone, possibly including the murderer, thought it was Ellen — but it wasn't. It was just some

158

small, dark-haired street girl who'd probably come down the alley to make money out of the stage-door johnnies.'

'Oh no!'

'Yes. She looked so much like Ellen in the gloom, but when she was brought into the light they could see it was someone else. Her hair was naturally black and she really was barely more than a child. The police are struggling to find out her name or anyone who cares that she's gone. Poor girl, just another young woman lost in the city.'

I put my head in my hands and James stroked my hair.

'Hello James!' said Margaret, bouncing into the room. 'Can I see where you were strangled?'

'Katherine,' said Aunt Alice from the threshold. 'May I have a word?'

She and I stood in the hallway and perused each other.

'You shouldn't let Mr King be so intimate. You are not engaged.'

'Oh, Aunt Alice. Can't you trust us? You can see he's not well. He should have someone to look after him, but he only has a charlady.'

'How do you know that?'

'He told me.'

'He can't stay here. A head injury won't necessarily stop improper advances.' Aunt Alice's narrowed eyes dared me to ask how she knew this was true.

'I fought the assailant off with all my might,' James was telling Margaret loudly. 'It takes more than a little strangulation to keep me down. I'm feeling much better now.'

'See,' hissed Aunt Alice. 'He's quite ready to . . . to…' She blushed.

I mentally cursed James for not helping.

159

'Besides, where could he stay precisely?' she went on. 'We have no spare bedrooms. You are crammed into an attic room with Connie.'

'If you recall, before Father disappeared, two maids were "crammed" into that room and no-one thought it unreasonable. We are absolutely fine.'

'It's not what Connie's used to.'

'Well…' I restrained the words I'd learned since being at the music hall. 'It'll do her good. James could stay in Father's study. I'm sure we could make a bed up on the couch in there. If you insist, perhaps we could make Ada lie on the threshold so that I can't be lured inside without a chaperone.'

For a moment we both boggled at this image and how we'd achieve it. We calmed down.

'I worry about whether he is . . . serious,' said Aunt Alice.

'Is that it?'

'Yes.' She looked down. 'I know I'm not your mother but I don't want your heart broken again.'

I gave her a small hug. 'If you mean Henry,' I said, 'it wasn't broken, just bruised. He released me from any understanding, and there wasn't really one in the first place.'

'But James…'

'I can't explain it, but can't you trust me? And him.'

'Even though you went out and found him the other night.'

I gasped. 'How did you know?'

'I didn't. I guessed. Oh Katherine.'

I wished everyone would stop saying that.

'Is this to do with that poor girl they found round the

160

corner?'

'Yes. Partly.'

'And having a man here might keep you safe.'

'Yes. Definitely.'

'I miss his moustache,' said Aunt Alice. She twinkled a little. 'Kissing a man without a moustache is like having coffee without cream. Or so they say. I'm going for a cycle with Margaret and Miss Robson. I am fairly sure that at this precise moment James has no plans for seduction, so I'll leave you be.' She paused and bit her lip. 'I'm not heartless, Katherine. You forget I was not much older than you are now when I came to live with you. I am not old now. You seem to think I've never had a sweetheart, or had anyone say "no" to me, or had to say "no" to someone else. I'll think about what you've said.'

She reached for her hat and I touched her arm. 'Don't ever feel you're not as good as Mother,' I said. 'I know you care just as much. I couldn't have asked for anyone better to look after us.'

Her eyes glistened but she kissed my cheek before turning to look in the mirror. 'Go on with you,' she said.

I waited in the drawing room with James until the cycling party had gone. 'What was all that whispering?' he said.

'I've asked if you can stay here to be nursed.'

'By you? All night?'

'Until you're better. And no, I'm sure your brow isn't so fevered that I need to mop it all night.'

'It is. Honestly.' James feigned a faint.

'You'll have to mop your own head. I need my beauty sleep.'

'True.'

I slapped his knee. From the kitchen came the smell of baking. James leant close. For all his nonsense, he didn't seem quite himself. Laying his head on my shoulder, he said, 'I've arranged to go to my aunt's at Kensington for a few days so *your* aunt needn't worry.'

'Oh.'

'I'm not altogether sure about your nursing skills,' he added. 'You tend to gallivant when you're bored. But I'm hoping you'll get many more chances to nurse me. I don't mean I'm hoping to be ill, but I… Anyway, what I mean is, Aunt Penelope has plenty of servants to look after me. My neck still feels as if it's almost severed. But if you insist, I could lie here if you'll do the seducing.' He kissed my neck and put his arm around my waist. 'Though I prefer you without a corset.'

'I don't know how you knew I wasn't wearing one, given that you were half dead.'

'Psychic powers. Perhaps you should include me in your act… Katherine, that was a joke. Stop sniggering. It's very unladylike.' He sat up and took my hand. His face was serious. 'Is there any point in asking you to stay home from the music hall tonight?'

His hand in mine felt strong. Even grey and tired, I could see he wanted to protect me with everything he had.

'No,' I said, 'there's no point. Connie and I said we'd be there early to go through a new routine, in the hope that someone will tell us what they wouldn't tell the police. Do you think we could go to Covent Garden now, in the daylight? Could you face it again? I'm sure there's something we can find out there if we ask the right people.'

James groaned. 'What with the assault and the heat, my head is killing me. But at least it's only my head and not

162

some maniac intent on slaughtering show girls. Very well, lead on Macduff. Unless you're sure you wouldn't rather seduce me instead.'

'I'd much rather,' I said, before I could stop myself. 'But I don't want there to be any more murders. It has to end.'

***

Covent Garden was so different in daytime that it might as well have been another place entirely. Men in bowler hats with barrows and crates thronged everywhere. There was a kind of beauty to the dance they performed, wheeling in and out with huge burdens yet never colliding, never dropping anything. All the same, their language was enough to make even Mabel blink.

'We'll have missed the rush,' said James. 'Most of the florists and greengrocers come at dawn. It's fairly quiet now.'

Quiet? It was heaving. The sun was doing its best through thick smog to scorch and suck the air away. I had felt brazen going out without a jacket, but now I was glad; the press of people and the heat reflected off the buildings around us made me feel as if I'd been dropped into an oven.

Near the theatre, people thronged to look at the latest posters and announcements. Some of the best singers performed here, and there was to be a grand concert later in the summer. James and I entered an alley and found the stage door.

'You're becoming far too familiar with this sort of life,' he murmured. 'I'd prefer to think of you at home tatting.'

'Do you even know what tatting is?'

'No, but it has to be safer than this.'

163

'Probably not the way I do it.'

The door was open in a vain attempt to ventilate. I stepped into the dark, fuggy interior and made my way down the corridor. This was far larger and fancier than the Merrymakers. The best singers had separate dressing rooms and one room was labelled *Wardrobe*. I could hear people within, and I opened the door.

Two women stared at us. They were surrounded with a rainbow of colour, a star burst of sparkle, a waterfall of lace.

'Good morning,' I said.

One of the women took pins from her mouth and jabbed them into a pin cushion in her wrist.

'Morning,' she said, glancing between us with a frown. 'Theatre's not open. Tickets round the front.'

'I know,' I said. 'It's not why we've come. I wanted to ask about someone who worked here a few years ago.'

'Lots come and go,' said the seamstress. 'It's 'ard work looking after this stuff. Not many 'ave the stamina.'

'I think she may have left to have a baby.'

Both women snorted. One nodded towards a basket in the corner where a wizened infant dozed.

'Or perhaps for another reason.'

'Well then, 'oo? We've got work to do.'

'Helen Henderson.'

Both women shrugged.

''Elen Brown,' said James.

There was a pause as the women glanced at each other. After a moment one of them spoke. 'Oh. Her.'

***

'So,' I said to Connie in the dressing room of the Merrymakers that evening, 'it seems someone in

164

management heard Ellen in the wardrobe room one day, singing a song from the show. The rest should have been history.'

'What do you mean?'

'I mean, she was offered the chance to train up for the opera. Her voice was that good. There was a bit of a mixed reaction from her colleagues. Some were pleased for her, others jealous.'

'They told you that?'

'Not exactly, but it pretty much summed up the reaction of the two we spoke to.'

'You said "*should* have been history".'

I paused, hairpins in my mouth the way the seamstresses had had dressmaking pins. In the mirror my face was rosy from an easy life and good food. Thinking of the two hard, wiry women in that wardrobe room, hollow-cheeked and narrow-eyed, and the baby in the corner, settled periodically with a drop of some potion in a bottle of grey-looking milk, I felt soft and pampered.

'Caleb didn't like it, apparently. He said she was getting above herself, that he wasn't having her go off with someone else. He went to the theatre one day and smashed things up, including Ellen. Or at least, he blacked her eyes and punched her about. He didn't break any limbs. She needed her hands to make a living. But after the beating she lost the baby she was expecting.'

Connie winced, as I had when they told me. 'It wasn't the first she'd lost. But despite that, she went back to him, and as far as they knew, to seamstressing, but not at their theatre. No-one could prove Caleb had done the damage because someone said he'd been elsewhere when it happened, just like the night Sally died. And Ellen wasn't saying anything, One of the women said that not long after, she heard that Caleb had got Ellen in the family way, but this time Ellen left Caleb and was never seen again. That's it. That was all they knew. Poor Ellen. And he's out there now, still trying to get to her.'

'We have to stop him,' said Connie, wiping her eyes. 'It's why we're here. We *can't* fail.'

'Oh gawd.'

The voice made us jump. It was Betty. She must have been eavesdropping. Tears were running down her face.

'I dint know that's why you was 'ere,' she said. 'I thought you was playing some silly game like what ladies do sometimes when they're bored. I dint know you was trying to find Ellen. I mean, I thought she was a bit stuck up, but now I can see why. I knew somefink, but never all that. If I'd known what you was trying to do, I'd a never…'

'Never what?'

'Never sent you them notes. The ones telling you to get lost.' She hesitated, half in, half out of the door.

'Did you send the flowers too?' said Connie.

'Flars? Me? I can't afford flars. It was just the notes. I'm real sorry. I'll get my things and go. Mr Templeton won't want me 'ere now.'

'Don't leave,' I said. 'I'm sorry you thought we were trying to take your jobs. You said you know something. Can you tell us what? Can you get the other girls to tell? Please, Betty. It could be the difference between life and death.'

166

CHAPTER 21
Connie

'Promise not to tell,' murmured Betty, uneasily.

'Of course we do,' said Katherine.

'I mean reelly promise. Cross my 'eart, 'ope to die. Both of yer.'

We did as we were told.

Betty leaned in. 'I knew she was married,' she whispered, 'an' she had a child, a little girl. I caught her looking at a little picture one day, see, and she owned up to it. Made me swear never to say nothing. She said it was because it would, what was it, "affect her stage act".' Betty sighed. 'I asked about 'er 'usband and she said he weren't around no more. I took that to mean 'e'd scarpered.'

'Do you know where she is now?' I asked.

Again, the same furtive glance. 'She was lodging down the street, in a back room at Doyle's. I went round sometimes. I don't know where the child was, but it weren't there. I used to chaff her, before I knew, that she could afford much better digs on two pound ten a week.' She rubbed her eyes, briskly. 'I went round after she sent that letter in, but she'd packed up an' gone. Old Doyle was furious, said she owed a week's rent.'

Katherine sighed. 'So we can't reach her.'

'We couldn't anyway,' I said. 'It's too much of a risk, with *him* still at large. What if we did find her, and we led him there as well?' I shuddered, and pulled my shawl closer round me.

I had spent much of the morning alone. Katherine was nursing James, and I didn't think they'd appreciate a third party being there. Besides, I might well have burst into tears at any show of affection. Albert had sent no word, no explanation for his absence the previous night. So I stayed in Katherine's little room, thinking over what had happened and how we could catch Caleb Brown. For I was sure he was behind it all.

I had considered wiring Albert to tell him what had happened, but then I imagined him ripping open the envelope, his eyes skimming the contents, and casting it aside. I composed a wire to Chief Inspector Barnes instead: *Girl murdered near Merrymakers last night had strong resemblance to Ellen Howe, Brown's missing wife STOP Reply to Demeray please STOP Swift.*

The reply was curt: *One mistake forgivable two foolish STOP will bear in mind Barnes.*

We were on our own. But not as much as poor Ellen must be.

'Wait,' I said to Betty. 'We received a note from Ellen a few days ago, in a pink envelope . . . did you deliver it?'

Betty nodded, biting her lip. 'It was waiting at my lodgings one evening when I got back from 'ere. It 'ad come by evening post. Just the envelope, with a piece of notepaper saying please deliver to Miss Caster. I never knew it was from Ellen, ain't never seen her writing. I thought I might as well deliver it, seeing as I had a note of my own to send you.'

'Do you have the envelope it came in?' I asked. 'We could check the postmark.'

Betty looked down. 'Burnt it,' she muttered.

Katherine put her head in her hands. 'It feels as if we're being thwarted at every turn,' she said, slightly muffled.

'But how did Ellen know we were looking for her?' I asked. 'You haven't told her, because you don't know where she is. Would any of the others know?'

Betty shook her head. 'Doubt it,' she said. 'I'm probably the nearest thing she 'ad to a friend.'

'I don't think she's far away,' I said, 'and that worries me. It means she isn't out of danger.'

Betty shivered. 'It makes we worry we'll all be murdered in our beds.' She stood up. 'I'm bringin' Buster in. I don't want him left outside in case something 'appens.'

Katherine and I looked at each other. 'So much for the information,' she said, softly.

'She tried to help,' I said. 'And at least she did give us Ellen's note.'

'Mm.' Katherine went to the costume rail. 'Tartan or stripes, tartan or stripes, oh I can't decide…'

'You sound like a music-hall song,' I said. 'Who do you think will squire us tonight; James, Tredwell or Dinsdale?'

'Perhaps all three,' said Katherine, returning with the striped dress and a clashing petticoat. 'I'd better look my very best.' Then she looked at me properly. 'Oh Connie, what is it?'

'He won't come, will he?' I choked out.

Katherine gave me a one-armed hug. 'I'm sure he'll try.'

But it was no good. The hug had opened the floodgates. Katherine tried to console me, but she might as well have tried to build a dam with toothpicks. Eventually I could cry no more and I sniffled myself into silence, dabbing at my eyes with my sodden handkerchief. I made the mistake of looking up, and the sight of myself in the dressing-table mirror almost set me off again. My face was blotchy, my eyes swollen, and my nose seemed to be twice its usual size.

I groaned as someone banged on the door. 'Gotta wire,' shouted Ron.

'I wonder who it is this time,' said Katherine, threading her way through the chairs and rails. 'Maybe someone else wants to warn me off.' She opened the door and held out a hand.

'Tain't for you,' said Ron. 'It's for the other one.'

I looked up, doubtfully. 'Me?'

'Yes you, miss,' said Ron. 'You look like you need cheering up,' he said, not unkindly.

I got up and took the envelope. I sat back down and looked at it for a while before sliding my thumb under the flap.

Called earlier but missed you STOP Miss you STOP See you at show A

I looked up to find both Ron and Katherine regarding me with curiosity. 'Is it good news, miss?' asked Ron. 'I can't tell.'

'Yes, Ron,' I said. 'It's very good news.'

***

'It's nice to see you looking brighter,' said Katherine. 'I

was starting to think you'd float away on your own tears, like Alice.' She turned to the mirror and drew on an eyebrow. 'I wonder if he'll come tonight.'

'Who?'

Katherine drew on her other eyebrow and raised them both. 'Caleb Brown. There's no reason for him to be here now.'

'That's true,' I said. 'He thinks he's killed Ellen.'

'He probably does,' said Katherine. 'That poor girl looked enough like her to fool everyone here, until they got her into the light.'

'He thinks he's won,' I said. 'He's paid her back for leaving him. He's probably arranged another alibi.' My hand crumpled the telegram.

'He hasn't won,' said Katherine. 'But what if he's found out it wasn't Ellen?'

'He'll still need an alibi. But maybe he'll think he's scared her off.'

Katherine still looked doubtful. 'You know,' she said slowly, 'I think he'll come. I have a feeling he'd want to make sure. But I have no idea how we'll catch him.'

For a moment I imagined Katherine, as Felicity, dangling on the end of a giant fishing rod. Then I gasped. 'I'm an idiot,' I said. 'And so are you. But you're the idiot we need.'

'I beg your pardon?' Katherine raised one black brow.

'What time is it?' I consulted my watch. 'Good, we still have an hour till curtain-up.'

'It would be lovely if you'd tell me what's going on in your mind,' Katherine said, plaintively.

The other performers were coming in now, still quiet and subdued after yesterday's events. I went to the costume

171

rail, found what I was looking for, and dropped it into Katherine's lap. She looked up at me, and beneath the paint, comprehension dawned. 'We're going to reel him in,' she said, holding the polka-dot dress up against herself.

'We must go and see Mr Templeton,' I said.

'*For one night only*,' whispered Katherine, her eyes as bright as stars. '*Little Dottie Jones*.'

***

'You're mad, the pair of yer,' Mr Templeton said crisply, biting the end off a cigar. 'You're gonna get yourselves killed.'

'No we won't,' said Katherine. 'There'll be people in the audience watching out for us. The minute he tries anything, they'll grab him. Think about it,' she wheedled. 'Once he's caught, Ellen can return, and you'll have your star.'

'And you'll need her,' I added, 'because tomorrow night's our last performance.'

'Ain't you two never heard of notice?' he demanded. 'I ought to dock your pay.'

'You'd better get your playbills printed up for tomorrow, then,' said Katherine. 'I'm sure Betty will be able to fill in next week.'

'It might draw a crowd,' he said thoughtfully. 'Although if anyone gets murdered —'

'So that's a yes?' Katherine leaned forward.

Mr Templeton scratched his head. 'Don't think I 'ave much choice. Now go and get yourself ready, F'licity, like a good girl.'

***

'I can't see him anywhere,' I said, peeping round the curtain at the packed house. 'Tredwell's there, in the

172

middle. No sign of Caleb Brown.' *He said he'd see me at the show.* I hoped Katherine couldn't hear the disappointment in my voice.

'Well, at least Tredwell can give us a lift home,' said Katherine, joining me. 'Maybe Albert's taken a box. So long as he hasn't come in evening dress again.'

'Not this time,' said a voice behind us, and I squealed. There, lounging in the wings with hands in pockets, was Albert, sporting a straggly brown wig along with Tredwell's clothes. 'Reg let me in and, um, provided the hair. I don't particularly want your man to spot me in the audience, given the state of King.'

'Did James get off safely?' Katherine asked, her face anxious.

Albert nodded. 'I accompanied him to Kensington. I'm not sure he'll stay there, though.'

'No,' said Katherine. 'He probably won't when he hears our plan.'

'Oh lord,' said Albert. 'What now?'

Applause broke out in front of the curtain and we had to jump back into the wings before it lifted. 'And noooww,' intoned Mr Templeton, 'Felicity Velour!'

Dan Datchett lumbered past. 'Tough crowd,' he said, out of the side of his mouth.

'Go on, Felicity,' said Albert, 'give 'em what for.'

'Thank you,' smirked Katherine, and pranced on stage to cheers.

'No flowers tonight?' asked Albert. 'No notes?'

'Only from you,' I said, and his arms slid around my waist.

'I'm sorry I was . . . distracted,' he murmured in my ear. 'I had some things to do that couldn't wait.'

173

'What sort of things?' I whispered.

'You'll miss your cue,' he muttered, and kissed my cheek. 'I'll tell you when I can. What's this plan you two have cooked up?'

The opening chords of our first number scraped out. I twisted round and kissed Albert on the lips. 'I'll tell you when I can.'

CHAPTER 22
Katherine

Dan Datchett had been right. It was a tough crowd. Whether it was ghouls brought out by the murder, or the heat, it was hard to say. I came off stage trembling even though I hadn't been sure if anyone was lurking in the audience.

'I ain't doing the ventriloquiz tonight,' said Mr Templeton. 'That's one ugly crowd and my throat's playing up. I got a new bloke with a mind-reading act I promised I'd try after the interval. Maybe it'll settle them down. You two can go early. 'Ere! Who's that?'

A shadow was moving swiftly towards us.

'Oh,' said Mr Templeton, 'it's Sir Galahad. Mighta guessed.'

'Nice dress, Katherine,' said James. 'Shame it couldn't have been brighter.'

I kicked him gently. 'That's my girl,' he whispered.

'I thought you were in Kensington,' said Connie. She was shaking too.

'Do you seriously think I'd leave Katherine?' said

James. 'Or you? Lamont needs all the help he can get managing you two.'

'I'm not sure if Caleb was out there.'

'Mmm. I'm sure he was. Lamont is out front trying to intercept him, but there are too many people about and too many doors.

'You're right,' said Albert, appearing and gathering Connie into his arms. 'If he was here, he's gone.'

'Gawd,' said Mr Templeton, 'will you two take your women away?'

'We'll be back tomorrow,' I promised.

'Yeah well, you're a draw, I gotta say, but that doesn't mean I'm happy.'

'We have to flush Caleb out,' I said. 'We have to help Ellen. It's why you hired us, remember.'

'You're gonna get yourselves killed and it's not the kinda publicity I want. Like I said, you've got your hands full, Sir Galahad, and I don't envy you.'

James grinned. 'Right, you painted trollop, put your own clothes on and let's go. There's another exit. Reg and I rounded up some lads to watch the stage door. There's only so much we can do to protect the other girls, but it's a start. Let's go home.'

'Which one?' said Connie.

'Father will disown me if I turn up with you lot again,' said Albert.

'We'll go to Kensington,' said James. 'Aunt Penelope won't interfere, and then we can get Katherine and Connie home.'

* * *

We sat in the Kensington garden and talked in low voices. If we'd hoped it might be cooler away from the

176

centre of town, we were mistaken. My temples felt as if they were being crushed. James ran his finger round his collar. I reached over to undo his tie and collar stud.

'Steady on, K,' said Albert.

'It's so hot,' I said, 'and it's hurting his neck.'

'As long as that's all you're doing.'

'Are you my father? You look after your own behaviour.'

He moved his hand from Connie's knee and scowled in the candlelight.

'Besides,' I said. 'I want you to listen. We've got a plan.'

'Why is my headache getting worse?' groaned James.

'K,' said Albert, 'you have been getting me into scrapes since we were three. It wasn't so bad when it ended up with nothing worse than a few grazes and no jam for tea. But we're grown up now. This isn't like climbing trees and pelting my brothers with berries.'

'It's not funny, Albert.'

'I know. I wasn't trying to be funny. It's not just you that I'm worried about, it's Connie. She's my responsibility.' He put his arm round her.

'It's our plan,' I said. 'Mine and Connie's. We need each other. But we also need your help. Yours and James's.'

'It's all right,' said Connie. 'With you two, this will work. I know it will.'

'All this for a girl you've barely met, who doesn't want your help, who doesn't even seem like a real person,' said Albert.

'She's real,' said Connie. 'You heard what Katherine and James found out. That makes her very real. And what I

177

haven't had a chance to tell you is that Mabel, the one with the blonde curls and the colourful language, came and had a chat to me while Katherine was changing.'

'I say,' said Albert, 'I hope you haven't learnt any bad words.'

Connie shrugged his arm off and rolled her eyes as if he was an idiot. 'Albert, she didn't come to teach me how to swear and if she did, does that matter? You know perfectly well I have plenty of self-control.'

He grunted.

'What did Mabel say?' I asked.

'She said that she'd met Ellen in Covent Garden years ago. They were like chalk and cheese, so people thought they didn't get on. That's partly how Ellen managed to keep hidden. Mabel sheltered her in the first place, after she'd left Caleb. Caleb didn't encourage the friendship and they lost touch.'

'That doesn't explain much that we didn't know,' said James.

'Listen. One night she met Ellen outside the theatre. Ellen was in a terrible state. She'd asked for a second chance on stage and been turned away. Her eyes had been blacked and she was clearly expecting again. She told Mabel she couldn't face losing another child but had nowhere to go. Mabel was about to move to the Merrymakers, and took Ellen with her to Lambeth. She said it was hard going, but Ellen took in a bit of sewing and helped with the neighbours' laundry, so she had a bit of spare cash to return to Somerset and have the baby. No-one thought it would live and Ellen wanted to bury it in the country.'

'But she came back,' said Albert.

'Yes. About three months later, Ellen knocked on Mabel's door. She said the baby had survived but there was no work for Ellen that could support them both. She asked if Mabel could help her get a job at the music hall.'

'And she auditioned and got the part of Little Dottie Jones,' I said.

'No,' said Connie. 'I mean, she auditioned and Mr Templeton thought he could make something of her. A straight-up singing act. Sentimental ballads, maybe one or two comic songs. Mabel said Ellen was beside herself. It was the chance she'd dreamed of and there'd be enough money to send home to the baby. But one day, on the other side of the Thames, she thought she saw Caleb, and was afraid he might have seen her. So she decided to disguise herself. She couldn't disguise her height, but she could disguise everything else, from her hair colour to her apparent age. A child performer. Caleb wasn't looking for a child. He was looking for a grown woman.'

'Oh,' I said. 'Now the act makes sense.'

'Yes. Everything was fine until one night she saw Caleb in the audience. This time she could see that he realised who she was. And she knew that if he got hold of her, he would kill her. So Ellen disappeared and this time, she didn't tell Mabel where she'd gone.'

I clutched at my hair. 'Why couldn't Mabel have told us this before?' I wailed.

Connie grimaced. 'She thought we might be from some sort of moral brigade, trying to reconcile Ellen with Caleb.' I looked at her. 'Yes, I know.'

We sat in the stifling garden in silence.

'Then our plan has to work,' I said. 'I shall dress as Dottie and go on stage, and Caleb will come for her.'

'I can't let you,' said James.

'It's our only chance. He was clever enough to have an alibi the night you and Sally were attacked. We need to draw him out.'

'I can't let you,' he repeated. I wanted to tell him that it was not up to him, but his tired face in the low light tugged at my heart.

'Connie, will you come for a turn in the garden?' Albert asked. They rose and walked into the gloom, slightly apart.

'James…'

'You're going to say I have no right to tell you what to do.' It wasn't like him to be so serious. 'You're going to say that you will do as you please, but Katherine, this is ridiculously dangerous. It's a matter for the police.'

'Who don't believe us. Besides, can you imagine some great clodhopping officer dressing up as Little Dottie Jones?'

I expected him to laugh, but he didn't. 'Katherine, I…'

I waited. Nothing more was said. A memory struggled through my headache. 'James, what did you mean when you said I'd have plenty more times to nurse you?'

'You know what I meant.'

'No. I don't.'

'Katherine, you are the most exasperating, stubborn, secretive, irritating, short woman I've ever had the misfortune to meet.'

'I'll bet I'm not.'

'Maybe not the shortest. But I don't want you harmed.'

'Why not?'

He sat silently for a few more moments, loosening his collar further and peering into the garden. Connie and Albert were too far into the darkness to see. The air was like treacle.

'I asked about Henry.'

'You explained all that.'

Another pause. 'I wasn't sure if you really cared about me.'

My face burned. I thought of the kisses we'd shared. Aunt Alice was right. What kind of woman did he think I was? Wasn't it obvious how I felt?

'I'm sorry,' he said, 'I shouldn't have mentioned it. I just want you to know that I am afraid for you. Very afraid.'

'I'll still do it,' I said. 'Whether you approve or not.'

'Oh, Katherine.'

A flash of lightning lit up the garden for one second. I blinked, and thunder rumbled.

Then the rain came down. Heavy, cool, blessed rain.

James hauled me under the veranda. The rain had soaked through my blouse and my hair was starting to frizz.

'I'll still do it,' I said. 'But I'd just like to say that I only kiss people I care for very much.'

He hadn't let me go. Another flash of lightning illuminated Albert and Connie running across the grass.

'Me too,' he said into my hair, 'Me too. It's why I wish you wouldn't do it. But if you won't stop, then you should listen. I have an idea.'

CHAPTER 23
Connie

Despite the fresh air at Kensington, and a mug of cocoa before bed, I slept badly. I tried not to toss and turn in case I disturbed Katherine, until she sighed and I realised that she was awake, too.

'Are you all right?' I whispered.

'I just hope we succeed,' she whispered back.

Not *I. We.*

'Of course we shall. Two more performances, and we're free.'

She was silent.

'Will you miss it, Katherine?'

She propped herself on an elbow, considering. 'I suppose I shall. The music hall has been so — different from my everyday life. I've spent so long keeping my head down and fitting in. I'm not sure how easy that will be after . . . after Felicity.' She snorted. 'I should probably thank her.' She reached for my hand. 'What about you, Connie?'

'I've wondered what it would be like doing what you

do,' I admitted. 'But I'm happier being the voice behind the scenes. I don't think I'm cut out for stardom.'

'Oh, Connie…' She squeezed my hand. 'I couldn't have done it without you. One more day, and everything will be back to normal.'

'I hope so,' I said. 'I really hope so.'

***

I struggled out of bed in the morning. I would have loved to sleep in and take my breakfast in bed; but that was not an option at the Demerays', and Albert had warned me the night before that he would call for me at nine o'clock sharp.

'Why?' I asked.

He smiled, provokingly. 'It isn't up to me to say.' His finger found the gap between glove and sleeve. 'I'll see you tomorrow.'

I was ready and waiting in the hall at five minutes to nine, and the bell rang a moment later. Ada opened the door to Albert, top-hatted, frock-coated, and looking rather nervous. The self-possession of the previous evening was gone entirely. 'Good morning, Master Bertie,' she remarked. 'You look as if you're off to your own funeral.'

'Lovely to see you too, Ada,' he replied. 'Shall we, Miss Swift?'

'Where are we going?' I asked, as the carriage bumped on the cobbles.

'To Coutts,' he said. 'But not for business this time.' He looked out of the window. 'I've had quite enough business lately.'

'I imagine you have,' I replied, thinking of his recent abstraction; how withdrawn and cold he had seemed. 'Are the new investments doing well?'

183

'We're almost there.'

The same flunkey rushed forward to meet us. 'Mr Lamont!' he cried, extending a hand.

Albert shook it firmly, then leaned forward and murmured in his ear. The flunkey listened, and an expression of incomprehension came over his face. 'If you're sure,' he said.

'It is all in order,' said Albert. 'Can you find me somewhere to wait?'

I wheeled round. 'Albert, what's going on?'

He beckoned me closer, and his breath tickled my ear. 'I said I'd tell you when I could. Don't worry, Connie.'

My anxiety did not diminish as the official led me down the corridor that Albert and I had walked down on our last visit. I wanted to turn and run; but I had a distinct feeling that something worse would happen if I did. 'Here we are,' said the flunkey, pausing at Mr Anstruther's door and knocking.

'Come in,' said a voice that was not Mr Anstruther's. But it was very familiar.

The flunkey opened the door, and bowed me in.

And there, sitting in one of the chairs, was Father.

'I expect you're wondering why I'm here, Connie,' he observed.

I could only stammer in reply. How did he know I wasn't in Brighton? Why had Albert delivered me to the bank? My face burned, and I put my hands to my cheeks to try and cool myself down.

'Do take a seat,' he said, and I collapsed into the nearest. 'You're not the one in trouble, Connie.' The corner of his mouth turned up. 'Quite the reverse.'

'I — what? I mean pardon?' I goggled at him.

184

'Young Lamont has pulled me out of a hole,' he said. For a moment I imagined a complicated scenario with ropes and pulleys, before composing myself. 'He called on me at my club a few days ago. You'll know why.'

'To — to ask permission?' I ventured.

'Indeed.' Father leaned forward. 'I must admit I didn't know much of the chap, I just assumed he was a hanger-on. Your mother doesn't speak well of him.' He grimaced. 'But he seemed eminently sensible. Particularly when we discussed circumstances. We got talking, and he advised me to be cautious with copper.' He puffed out a breath. 'Thought he was trying to impress me, and laughed it off. Should have listened. Bad crash.'

'How — how bad?' I quavered.

'Bad enough. But he wired me the minute he heard, and offered to help. I think between me and his father, he's been pretty caught up. He spent most of Thursday with us, drawing up a plan.'

'His father?'

'Yes.' Again, the rueful smile. 'Another old man who doesn't know when to stop. I gather Lamont manages most of it, which is as well.'

'But — why didn't Albert tell me himself?'

'I asked him if he'd let me do it.' Father examined his fingernails. 'I have a feeling,' he said softly, 'that this young man of yours would play it down. But you ought to know, Connie, that I am very happy with your choice.' He leaned forward and took my hand. 'As far as I'm concerned, you can marry tomorrow, if that's what you want.'

'I think it might take longer than that,' I said, beaming.

'Yes.' He smiled back, a little sadly. 'I gather that you

have some secret business on hand before you return to the bosom of the family tomorrow. I won't keep you from it.'

I rose, feeling dismissed. 'Thank you, Father,' I said, and withdrew, closing the door behind me.

It was a short walk to the room where Albert was waiting. He was alone, and I ran to him.

'I have so much to thank you for,' I murmured. 'I'm sorry I ever doubted you.'

He lifted my face to his. 'I'm sorry I couldn't be more open with you.' I put my head on his shoulder, and he held me close.

***

'You don't have any more surprises for me, do you?' I asked, as we sped along.

'Not of that kind,' he said. 'We need to call at Scotland Yard, though. If I could get every policeman in London into the hall tonight, I still wouldn't be satisfied.'

Albert and I handed our cards in at the desk, and a few minutes later we were ushered into the presence of Chief Inspector Barnes. A telegram lay on the desk.

'Well,' he said. 'It's you two.'

'I'm afraid so,' I replied.

'Glad to see you,' he said, rising and shaking hands. 'Had a chap in earlier, wanting to give a statement. He'd sworn blind that he was with Caleb Brown the night that young woman was strangled, and in a different part of town. But when he saw the report about the girl at Lambeth, he decided to come clean. Apparently he and Brown used to work together at Covent Garden before Brown lost his job. Brown asked if he'd vouch for him, so he could have a night out without his missus, if you know what I mean.'

'I know what you mean,' said Albert, grim-faced.

'So our man thought nothing of it, even when Brown asked again the next day. But two little women, as small as Caleb's missus... Two women dead in two days was too much for him.' His mouth twisted. 'One mistake forgivable, two foolish. Tell me what you need.'

***

The playbills outside the Merrymakers screamed out the news that Katherine had whispered the day before:

FOR ONE NIGHT ONLY!!!

LITTLE DOTTIE JONES!!!

'Do you feel ready?' I murmured, as we passed through the double doors an hour earlier than our usual time. There were various men loafing in the vicinity; but as I had already spotted the Chief Inspector on the steps, in a battered bowler and trousers with baggy knees, I felt reassured.

'I don't think I'll ever feel ready,' Katherine said, and the door banged to behind us.

Mr Templeton paced in the foyer. 'You're gonna do it, then,' he said, round his cigar.

Katherine drew herself up to her full height. 'We are,' she said.

He stopped, and surveyed the pair of us. 'They're all in. All the dancers, an' the acrobats. They'll look after yer best they can.' He hurried into his office, muttering something that sounded like 'Bloody maniacs.'

We walked to the dressing room like a pair of condemned women. I tried to calm myself. Albert and James would be there, and both were carrying pistols. The Chief Inspector and his men were on patrol. Albert had recruited the male servants, and, I suspected, some of his brothers to assist. But I was still shaking like a leaf when I walked into the dressing room.

A ragged cheer rang out. 'What kept yer?' Selina asked, putting a glass of brandy into my hand. 'Come on, let's get you ready.' She led me to a chair, and began to take out my hairpins.

'You don't need to,' I protested. 'I stand in the wings, you know that. No one sees me.'

'Don't matter,' said Betty, moving towards Katherine and picking up a brush. 'You help us, we help you. We're gonna get Ellen back, together.'

***

The matinee was our best performance so far. Katherine did two encores, and I suppose I did too. 'Don't forget!' she cried. 'Come and see Little Dottie Jones tonight! Don't miss it!'

The curtain fell for the final time, and we ran offstage. Reg was waiting in the wings. 'No sign,' he hissed. 'He ain't here yet.'

I looked at Katherine. 'Don't tell me he isn't coming. Not after all this.'

She took my arm and led me down the corridor. 'He's coming,' she said. 'He won't be able to keep away.' And as she led me to the dressing room, her step firm and unwavering, I wished that I could be so sure. So resolute.

CHAPTER 24
Katherine

The music hall was stifling. It was as if the previous night's rain had never happened. There was no fresh air outside, where the sky was thick with heat and smoke. Opening the doors would have made no difference even if Mr Templeton had allowed it. Beyond the footlights I could see the patrons moving in the smoky air, voices raised, bottles banging, ribald shouts aimed at the girls weaving in and out of the tables. I was glad Felicity Velour was not making an appearance. She was, after all, an exaggeration of myself, and tonight I felt unequal to dealing with the remarks she might attract. I didn't have the vocabulary, and in general I could only guess at what they meant. Given my naivety, tonight the costume of a little girl seemed oddly appropriate.

I looked down at my legs and felt more naked than I had without a corset. At least then there had been two layers of thick cotton between me and the world. Now I just had threadbare striped stockings.

Tonight I would be performing in Dottie's little-girl

outfit and a black wig which was attached so tightly that I feared I'd be stuck with it forever. I was not me tonight. I was not even a version of me. I nodded to the conductor and forced on a smile.

'Now who looks like Alice?' whispered Connie. It was meant to cheer me up, but I could see my own anxiety reflected in her face. Surely a strangler wouldn't adopt another mode of attack? He wouldn't produce a knife, or a gun...

'On the count of three,' I said out of the corner of my mouth.

'AAAAND back for a visit — iiiit's Little Dottie Jones!'

I skipped onto the stage. If anyone ever invents an international award for acting, I deserve it for that evening.

I heard grumbling about the singing. Connie's voice was not the same as Ellen's. Just as beautiful, but lower, and different in tone. It seemed wrong to be saucy while dressed as a child; my diffidence infuriated some and amused others. But by the time we started the second song, the grumbles had died away. Connie and I had won them over.

I kept scanning the auditorium. The smoke was so thick that I could not see past the second row of tables where the audience sang along and thumped the tables. In the shadows at the edges men were moving, smoking, drinking, pinching the good-time girls perhaps. One of them, I was sure, was watching me and me alone. No, there were two, one on either side, and as the act drew to a close the one on the right shifted out of sight. Perhaps I was imagining it. My head throbbed, the music blared in my ears, my own feet thumping across the stage made my bones hurt. The smoke and airless heat made my throat ache. The shadowy figure on the left was playing with something in his hands. A ribbon, a tie, a rope? As I finished a sentimental ballad about death, a slurring voice called out. 'Thought you was dead, Dottie. Thought they was picking you off one by one. Maybe the Ripper's back. Wot you reckon?'

There was a rumble of noise; part laughter, part disapproval, part fear.

'Stow it mate!' shouted another voice. 'Don't frighten the kid.'

'Garn, it's a joke! She can take it, can't yer love!'

'Oughter be dead,' said another voice, low and barely audible.

''Oo said that? That ain't funny, that ain't. Come on Dottie! Ignore 'em! Give us another chorus!'

I finished with a bow, my false hair dangling over my false smile, and tripped into the wings. I could not stop shaking.

Connie put her arms round me and I could feel her trembling too.

'You're right,' I said. 'Perhaps we should both have skipped lunch last November.'

'Yes,' she said. 'And right now I would be at a stultifying dinner with a prize bore talking about tigers and squeezing my knee, and you would be . . . what would you be doing?'

'She'd be tatting,' said James, putting his hand on my shoulder. 'I'd give you a hug too, Katherine, but I can see what the stuff on your face is doing to Connie's clothes, so I'll give it a miss for now.'

'James!' said Connie. 'I thought you were patrolling the

191

audience with Albert.'

'We think we know where Caleb is,' said James. 'We need to flush him out.'

'I don't think this is working,' said Connie. 'We thought he'd rush the stage, and he's just lurking. Perhaps you need to goad him, Katherine, and make him fly at you.'

'Actually,' said James, glancing between me and Mr Templeton, 'there's another plan.'

'Are you sure you're both up for it?' said Mr Templeton.

'What do you mean?' said Connie. 'I don't know what you're talking about. Up for what?'

I hugged her tighter, then stepped back.

'We've got a new ventriloquiz act,' said Mr Templeton. 'As if this weren't bad enough.' His words were wry but his face worried. His cigar had gone out.

'Stay in the wings, Connie. We need you as a witness.'

'What do you —'

I rushed to the changing room as the mind-reader went on stage. Five minutes later I was in the wings beside Mr Templeton, with the dummy's cap over the tucked-up wig, and a cloak covering me from the neck down. Connie gasped, then put her hands to her mouth. 'You look as if someone's —'

'Shh,' I hissed.

'Ready, love?' said Mr Templeton. 'Last chance to change yer mind.'

'Can't keep the audience waiting Mr T,' I said, and he lifted me up as if I were a doll.

***

'Evening ladies and gents! Will yer look at my pal. Wot

192

a state. Wot a state you're in, pal. Wot you been a-doing of?'

I shrugged as if I were made of wood, my arms and my bare legs angular.

'You bin playing in the coal cellar and rubbed yer eyes?'

I shook my head. My cap wobbled.

'You been fighting?'

I shook my head again and the hat waggled. I opened my mouth like a dummy and a soft West Country voice came from it.

'I bin hit.'

'You bin hit?' said Mr Templeton. 'I'll say. Look at them shiners. Yer eyes are as black as a chimney sweep's ar... arm. Who dun it?'

I shook my head and looked down.

'Gorn quiet on me 'ave yer? Was it someone you trusted? Don't you want to tell on him?'

The audience had started to rumble. Shifting their feet, audibly wondering what was coming next.

I moved my mouth and the West Country voice spoke. 'I did tell. No-one did nothing.'

'It's gonna take a magician to get things out of you today, ain't it? Too bad we haven't got one 'andy. What we need is the Great . . . the Great . . . what's his name?'

I leant my head against Mr Templeton as if I was tired, and whispered.

Mr Templeton boomed: 'The Great Mystericon!' There was a drum-roll, then a clash of cymbals.

'Did someone call?' I lifted my head and turned it as much like a puppet as I could. The drop of my mouth didn't have to be faked. James bounded up to me in shirt sleeves and purple trousers, wearing a black half-mask, a woollen scarf, his battered tramp's hat, and a waistcoat with a million blue sequins.

'Thank the Good Lord you're here,' said Mr Templeton without rising. 'Look at my pal, wot a state. Won't tell me nothing. Can you 'elp?'

James put his hands on his hips. 'Indeed I can!' He leaned forward and pushed his sleeves up, showing his empty hands to the audience. 'What's this?'

He leaned over and felt behind my ear. Our eyes met, and his look told me what his words never seemed to as his fingers brushed my skin.

'It's a wedding ring!' James held it aloft, and the audience applauded and cheered.

'Gawd, you don't want one of them!' yelled someone. 'Might as well find a shackle. Money, that's what's needed!'

'There's something else!' announced James, slipping his hand into Mr Templeton's jacket pocket. 'A belt! Did someone hit you with a belt?'

I nodded.

'And a fist, I'll be bound.'

I nodded again, and dropped my head.

'What's under your hat?'

James lifted my cap and pulled out three red carnations, and the black hair came tumbling down. 'Carnations — they mean heartbreak,' he said. 'Did your heart break, Dottie?' he said, and I nodded once more. I was glad that I didn't have to speak. Mr Templeton let me slip from his lap and as I stood up the cloak dropped from my shoulders. Underneath, I wore a loose dress.

'Is it because you lost three babies, Dottie? Was it

194

because you were hit? Who did it? Was it the same man who used something like this on Sally and on me, and on the poor girl who died outside this music hall?'

James's hand spun in the air and out of nowhere a piece of cord whirled over his head. Then he pulled off his scarf, revealing the bruises around his neck.

'You're safe now, Dottie. You're safe. You'll never see him again.'

There was a roar from the left of the stage. Chairs were overturned, glasses knocked from tables and smashed. A dark, stocky man leapt onto the stage, smashing one of the footlights, and grabbed my shoulder. His eyes were red, his teeth bared in a snarl.

'You bitch, you painted woman, you —' He raised his fist but before James or Mr Templeton could react, the dancers and the acrobats rushed from the wings and pushed him to the ground, kicking, punching, swearing.

'Ellen is one of us!'

'Sally was our friend!'

'That kid out in the alley never deserved —'

The police stormed the stage, and with James and Albert were trying to drag the women off Caleb Brown.

'STOP!'

The shout came from the wings.

Everything paused in a tableau. Betty's fist was raised, Selina's foot ready to kick, Mabel's mouth about to curse.

Ellen Howe walked to centre stage. Small, dainty, dressed as a woman, not a girl. She was hatless, and mouse-brown roots showed above the black dye.

'Give him to the police, girls,' she said.

'But Ellen, he don't deserve no mercy,' said Betty.

'Mercy's up to God,' said Ellen. 'Justice is up to us.

195

He's the one who's a savage. Not you.' She stepped up to the footlights and addressed the auditorium.

'That is my husband. He did that.' She pointed at me, standing alone with my two blackened eyes. 'I lost two kids. Maybe three. He made me lose all respect in myself. No man would help to protect me, or take any action against him. "You married him. It's what you chose," they said. "Marry a pig, learn to like pork," they said. So I run away. With my friend's help, I saved the next baby and I come back. But he wouldn't let me go, not he, and now he's got two murders to his name. If he'd had the chance, there'd have been a third tonight. I want the world to know what he done. And you…'

She pointed at James.

'I bet a gent like you knows one of them newspaper men. Get him to put the story in his paper. Maybe someone will think twice about striking their wife. Men like my husband don't deserve to be called men.' She turned to the Chief Inspector. 'They deserve to hang.'

CHAPTER 25
Connie

'What a beautiful day,' said Katherine. 'Just right for a bicycle ride into the country. I'm amazed at you, Connie, managing to be up and dressed so early.'

'Albert thought we should start early,' I said, adjusting my hat. 'Otherwise the heat will be oppressive.'

'True.' Katherine looked at herself in the glass. 'Although it isn't like Albert to get up early either. Still, at least we shall have plenty of time for lunch. Do I need to bring anything?'

'No,' I replied. 'Just yourself.'

The bell rang, and Ada bustled to the door with an excessive amount of shuffling and rustling. 'Now then,' she said. 'Both of you. I expect gentlemanly behaviour. After what I've heard and read, I'm not sure I ought to let the ladies out at all.'

We walked down the stairs to see Albert and James kitted out in cycling clothes. 'Got your divided skirts, ladies?' James enquired.

Ada huffed. 'Exactly,' she said, stamping off to the

kitchen. 'I don't know what the world is coming to.'

I caught Albert's eye, and smiled. 'Shall we?' he said.

'Yes.' He took my arm and led me down to the yard, where my steed was waiting.

***

In a few short miles we were out of noisy, grimy London, and able to talk freely as we cycled along the calm back roads. 'I gather circulation is up, King,' Albert commented, putting on a burst of speed to catch James.

'It certainly is,' said James. 'The paper's never done so well. And the publicity about Ellen has brought in several donations for women's charities and missions. Some small, some big, but all most welcome.'

'I don't think the publicity has harmed Ellen, either,' I remarked.

Katherine grinned. 'Mr Templeton wrote to me, care of Dr Farquhar, to express his thanks and gratitude. He even enclosed what he described as "a small 'onorarium". He said that after dealing with us, he's considering a lion taming act — I can't think what he means. But anyway, luncheon is on me.'

'Not this time, K,' said Albert, peering into the distance. 'I think we're a bit early for lunch, you know. Maybe we should make it elevenses, and push on.'

'How pretty it is.' Katherine's stockings flashed white as she drove the pedals and caught up with Albert. 'Like a picture postcard.' She looked over her shoulder at me. 'Bet you can't beat me Connie, despite your long legs.'

I took advantage of the gradual descent into the village to whizz past her, and Albert pedalled alongside me. 'No scorching, now,' James shouted. 'Riding too fast is unladylike.'

'Are you all right, Connie?' Albert asked, slowing down and looking across at me. 'You seem quiet.'

'Oh yes,' I said. 'I'm just enjoying the moment.' We gazed at the landscape before us; a patchwork of green fields, with cottages, an inn, and a little stone church at its heart.

***

We cycled to the inn and left our bicycles outside. Albert took my arm, then dropped it, then took it again. 'Make your mind up, Lamont,' called James. 'Are you or aren't you?'

'Oh, I am,' said Albert, squeezing tight. 'I most definitely am.'

The innkeeper hurried up to greet us. 'Lamont party? Excellent, excellent. Ladies, if you'll follow me.' I transferred my grip from Albert to Katherine, and followed him.

'What's going on?' Katherine asked, trying to pull away. 'How does he know Albert's name?'

'We've arranged a little surprise, Katherine,' I confided. 'We have two rooms booked at the inn.'

Katherine looked up into my face. 'A holiday?' she said, incredulously. 'But — well, that's rather modern.'

'We are sharing a room, and the men will be too.' I said, laughing. 'Given the things we've been doing lately, I thought you'd find it tame.'

'But — what about clothes, and luggage, and your maid? How long are we staying? I can't desert Dr Farquhar without notice, and James has the newspaper to think of.'

I smiled at her worried face. 'It's all in hand, Katherine.'

The innkeeper opened the door of a pretty low-ceilinged

room, with a view of the church and a vase of red roses in the window. It had two beds, and on each was laid an outfit. I had selected the cornflower-blue dress, beautifully finished by Maria. Katherine gasped at her transformed rose-pink dress, now with a matching bolero jacket fashioned out of the remains of her flounces. 'What — how —'

'I'll leave you to get ready,' said the innkeeper. 'Wouldn't do to be late, would it?' He winked, and withdrew.

Katherine rounded on me. 'Late for what?' she demanded. 'How did these dresses get here?'

'Tredwell brought them,' I said, closing the curtains. 'He's also brought morning suits for the men. I suggest you get changed, Katherine, or you'll never be ready in time.'

Katherine stared at me, frowning, then opened the curtains again and pointed at the church. I nodded, and the force of her hug nearly knocked me over.

***

'I wondered why your hair was so very fancy this morning,' Katherine said as we peeped out of the window, taking care not to crease ourselves.

'I thought I should take advantage of having a maid,' I said, touching the edifice of pins and waves with some trepidation. 'How I missed Mary. She wasn't very pleased with me this morning, though. "All this to go for a bicycle ride," she said.'

'I'm shocked,' said Katherine, looking anything but. 'This is the second time you've booked a hotel sneakily. You're as bad as Ellen. All that hunting for her, and she was at The Grosvenor in Victoria the whole time.'

'Which is much nicer than the hotel in Putney, and you

200

can't get more anonymous than a place where people are constantly coming and going,' I said. 'I wish I'd thought of it . . . although it was more fun at Albert's. Maybe we'd have found her a week earlier and I could have gone home. And speaking of home —'

The sound of hooves, and our carriage came into view. Hodgkins pulled up before the church, and Father got out, handing Mother down the steps. Even from this distance I could see her looking at the church critically. Her words floated up to us. 'It's very pretty, but I don't see why we've come all this way to look at it.' Hodgkins helped my sisters down, and they wandered listlessly after my parents.

'Oh my, Connie,' said Katherine, touching my arm. 'I can't imagine what your mother will say.'

A knock at the door. Katherine crossed the room and opened it, revealing James looking smart and almost serious, with a red rose in his buttonhole. 'Well,' I said, picking up my bouquet from the vase and shaking the water off, 'I think I'm about to find out.'

***

I barely remember anything of the ceremony. Father was waiting for me outside the church, his face a kaleidoscope of smiles and seriousness. 'You look lovely, Connie,' he said, giving me his arm. 'I'm very proud of you both.'

'Is Mother going to kill me?' I muttered under my breath.

He patted my hand. 'Not today.'

The *Wedding March* rang out as we entered the little church, and there was a flutter of aahs and sighs as light as butterfly wings, but I only had eyes for the altar steps, where Albert waited for me. I felt as if I were gliding towards him, pulled by an invisible thread that bound the pair of us. 'You look more beautiful than ever, Connie,' he murmured. 'I didn't think it was possible.'

There were responses, there must have been, from both of us, and I recall Albert taking my hand, and sliding the cool gold band onto my finger. After that everything was a blank until the vicar said 'I now pronounce you man and wife.' Albert bent his head to kiss me, and I never wanted it to end, though for propriety's sake I suppose it had to.

'How does it feel to be Mrs Lamont?' Albert asked, as we walked down the path to the inn, with Katherine and James behind us.

'Mrs Lamont,' I mused. 'Constance Lamont.'

'You sound like a romantic heroine,' said Katherine, laughing.

I smiled serenely. 'Perhaps I am today.' I looked up at Albert. 'Although being a romantic heroine does make one rather hungry.'

'I did arrange a wedding breakfast, dear.' Albert heaved a huge sigh, but the grin on his face gave him away. 'Is there anything else you require?'

I grinned back. 'Just undying devotion; nothing more.'

***

Mother made a beeline for me as soon as she entered the inn. 'Connie, dear,' she said, whisking over and planting a kiss on my cheek. 'This is a surprise.'

'Albert and I decided we would prefer a quiet wedding,' I said, feebly.

She gazed around the inn, taking in the heavy oak furniture and the flag-stoned floor. 'There's quiet, and there's quiet,' she said. 'At any rate you are married, and I have seen you sign the register, so the deed is done. I presume someone will put an announcement in the *Times*? Or are the pair of you intending to live as hermits?'

'Hardly, Mother.' I looked for Albert, but he was suspiciously deep in conversation with James.

'Perhaps I misjudged that young man,' Mother said, reflectively. 'Your father gives me to understand that he has been most helpful. Who knows, Connie, if he behaves himself perhaps we might take him into partnership in the firm one day.'

'Albert, or Father?' I asked, and hurried towards Katherine, who was being admired by Aunt Alice, Margaret and Ada.

'I do apologise, Miss Swi — Mrs Lamont, for my hasty words this morning,' Ada said, stepping forward and curtseying like a sort of automaton. 'I honestly thought shenanigans were in the offing.'

I smiled. 'They were, in a way,' I said.

'Oh no, I don't mind *these* sorts of shenanigans,' said Ada, laying a hand on my arm.

'Did someone say shenanigans?' James appeared out of nowhere and removed a sugared almond from behind Ada's ear. 'Can I join in?'

Ada giggled, then sobered up instantly. 'Not just yet, young man.' And she gave Katherine a meaningful look. 'You'll have to jump for that bouquet, Miss Kitty.'

***

Everyone gathered on the green to see us off. I had changed into my other dress, while Albert was in his travelling clothes. 'Where's Katherine?' I asked, looking around for her rose-pink dress.

'Where King is, I imagine,' said Albert. 'Look, by that copse of trees.' James, with his back to us, was talking earnestly to someone. I caught a glimpse of rose and a flash of auburn hair. He swept off his hat, and the pair vanished behind a tree.

'Oh, really.' But I couldn't help smiling. 'I suppose I should be thankful that he kept his speech short and proper.'

'Indeed,' said Albert. 'Another good reason to marry in haste.'

'So long as we don't repent at leisure,' I replied.

'As if that will ever happen,' said Albert, gathering me in his arms.

'AHEM,' said Mr Lamont loudly, and we jumped apart. 'If the happy couple wouldn't mind waiting a moment, we'll wave them off.'

Katherine and James sauntered over as if they had been sitting in Sunday school. 'Till the next adventure,' said James, shaking Albert's hand and kissing my cheek.

'Do you think we'll have any more adventures?' I asked Katherine, and suddenly I felt sad, in spite of the wonderful day.

'Of course we shall,' said Katherine, standing on tiptoe and hugging me. 'We'll always have adventures. I hope I get to wear nicer clothes in the next one.'

'I'm bringing Mary next time,' I said. 'Anyway, we have to have another adventure so that James can wear that beautiful waistcoat. I was rather disappointed that it didn't make an appearance today.'

'Oh, I'm saving it for later,' said James. 'It wouldn't do to wear it out.' Katherine dug him in the ribs, and murmured something which I suspected would have made Ada blush.

'Enough of your shenanigans,' said Albert, handing me

into the carriage. 'We've got our own adventure to undertake, and if we don't hurry Tredwell will leave without us.' He got in after me, closed the door, and we waved to our guests until we could see them no more.

'Thank heavens for that,' said Albert, pulling me towards him.

'For what?' I asked, putting my arms around his neck.

'I've been waiting all day, you know.' A little smile played on his lips as he gazed at me, and my heart skipped.

'For what?' I whispered.

'For everyone to stop looking at us,' he replied, turning up my chin. 'So that I can kiss you properly.' He bent his head, and I closed my eyes in anticipation of my second kiss as a married woman.

'Oh, Albert,' I murmured, 'it's a good thing no-one saw that kiss. You're doing it all wrong.'

He pulled away for a moment to look at me.

'It's true,' I assured him. 'That kiss was most improper. I think we need more practice.' And as the horses clattered along, we did our very best to get it right.

ACKNOWLEDGEMENTS

First of all, a big thank you to our beta readers — Ruth Cunliffe, Christine Downes, Stephen Lenhardt, and Val Portelli — and our very thorough proofreader, John Croall (we put that one typo in just for you!). Bows, curtsies, encores and flowers thrown on the stage for you all! As ever, any remaining errors are the responsibility of the authors (and it was always the other one's fault!).

One of our go-to places when doing the research for this book was the Victoria and Albert Museum's web resource about music hall and variety theatre: http://www.vam.ac.uk/page/m/music-hall/. Not only that, but the V&A Theatre & Performance Enquiry Service wrote back to us with some fascinating information about music-hall performers' wages. Thank you so much! We might have to write another music-hall book to make good use of it.

Our final thanks go to you, the reader. We hope you've enjoyed Connie and Katherine's foray into the world of the music hall, and if you could leave a short review of the book on Amazon or Goodreads it would be very much appreciated by both of us.

Font and Image Credits

Fonts:

Main cover font: Birmingham Titling by Paul Lloyd (freeware):
https://www.fontzillion.com/fonts/paul-lloyd/birmingham

Classic font: Libre Baskerville Italic by Impallari Type (http://www.impallari.com):
https://www.fontsquirrel.com/fonts/libre-baskerville
License — SIL Open Font License v.1.10:
http://scripts.sil.org/OFL

Vector graphics:

Theatre masks (recoloured) by OpenClipart Vectors:
https://pixabay.com/en/comedy-face-theater-tragedy-masks-157719/

Curtain (rescaled, cropped and recoloured) by Dieter_G:
https://pixabay.com/en/curtain-stage-theater-red-941716/

Ribbons on masks taken from Theatre Masks Clip Art by Ivo: http://www.clker.com/clipart-30136.html

Music stave vignette (photo cropped, background removed) by KateCox:
https://pixabay.com/en/notes-piano-sheet-music-keys-old-1422671/

Shoes vignette (cropped, recoloured, background removed and duplicated): Evening Slippers in the Metropolitan Museum of Art:
https://www.metmuseum.org/art/collection/search/168349

All images used are listed as public domain (CC0) at source.

Cover created using GIMP image editor: www.gimp.org.

About Paula Harmon

At her first job interview, Paula Harmon answered the question 'where do you see yourself in 10 years' with 'writing', as opposed to 'progressing in your company.' She didn't get that job. She tried teaching and realised the one thing the world did not need was another bad teacher. Somehow or other she subsequently ended up as a civil servant and if you need to know a form number, she is your woman.

Her short stories include dragons, angst ridden teenagers, portals and civil servants (though not all in the same story — yet). Perhaps all the life experience was worth it in the end.

Paula is a Chichester University English graduate. She is married with two children and lives in Dorset. She is currently working on a thriller, a humorous murder mystery and something set in an alternative universe. She's wondering where the housework fairies are, because the house is a mess and she can't think why.

Website: www.paulaharmondownes.wordpress.com
Amazon author page: http://viewAuthor.at/PHAuthorpage
Goodreads: https://goodreads.com/paula_harmon
Twitter: https://twitter.com/PaulaHarmon789

Books by Paula Harmon

Murder Britannica
When Lucretia's plan to become very rich is interrupted by a series of unexpected deaths, local wise-woman Tryssa starts to ask questions.

The Cluttering Discombobulator
Can everything be fixed with duct tape? Dad thinks so. The story of one man's battle against common sense and the family caught up in the chaos around him.

Kindling
Is everything quite how it seems? Secrets and mysteries, strangers and friends. Stories as varied and changing as British skies.

The Advent Calendar
Christmas as it really is, not the way the hype says it is (and sometimes how it might be) — stories for midwinter.

Weird and Peculiar Tales (with Val Portelli)
Short stories from this world and beyond.

ABOUT LIZ HEDGECOCK

Liz Hedgecock grew up in London, England, did an English degree, and then took forever to start writing. After several years working in the National Health Service, some short stories crept into the world. A few even won prizes. Then the stories started to grow longer . . .

Now Liz travels between the nineteenth and twenty-first centuries, murdering people. To be fair, she does usually clean up after herself.

Liz's reimaginings of Sherlock Holmes, her Pippa Parker cozy mystery series, and *Bitesize*, a collection of flash fiction, are available in ebook and paperback.

Liz lives in Cheshire with her husband and two sons, and when she's not writing or child-wrangling you can usually find her reading, messing about on Twitter, or cooing over stuff in museums and art galleries. That's her story, anyway, and she's sticking to it.

Website/blog: http://lizhedgecock.wordpress.com
Facebook: http://www.facebook.com/lizhedgecockwrites
Twitter: http://twitter.com/lizhedgecock
Goodreads: https://www.goodreads.com/lizhedgecock

Books by Liz Hedgecock

Short stories

The Secret Notebook of Sherlock Holmes
Bitesize

Halloween Sherlock series (novelettes)

The Case of the Snow-White Lady
Sherlock Holmes and the Deathly Fog
The Case of the Curious Cabinet

Sherlock & Jack series (novellas)

A Jar Of Thursday
Something Blue
A Phoenix Rises

Mrs Hudson & Sherlock Holmes series (novels)

A House Of Mirrors
In Sherlock's Shadow (2019)

Pippa Parker Mysteries (novels)

Murder At The Playgroup
Murder In The Choir
A Fete Worse Than Death
Murder In The Meadow

Caster & Fleet Mysteries (with Paula Harmon)

The Case of the Black Tulips
The Case of the Runaway Client
The Case of the Deceased Clerk
The Case of the Masquerade Mob

Printed in Poland
by Amazon Fulfillment
Poland Sp. z o.o., Wrocław

59342758R00129